CW00649448

NANCY WARREN

THE VAMPIRE BOOK CLUB

FIRST IN A PARANORMAL
COZY MYSTERY SERIES

The Vampire Book Club, Copyright © 2020 by Nancy Warren

Cover Design by Lou Harper of Cover Affairs

All rights reserved.

No part of this book may be reproduced in any form or by any electronic or mechanical means, including information storage and retrieval systems, without written permission from the author, except for the use of brief quotations in a book review.

Thank you for respecting the author's work.

ISBN: ebook 978-1-928145-82-0

ISBN: print 978-1-928145-81-3

Ambleside Publishing

INTRODUCTION

I was a divorced, middle-aged witch banished to Ireland. My life could be summed up in a limerick...

There once was a misguided witch
Who tried a man's fate to switch
Her punishment set
To Ireland she must get
But better than feathers and pitch!

With a name like Quinn Calahan I sounded as Irish as a leprechaun dancing a jig on a four leafed clover, but the truth was, I'd never been closer to the emerald isle than drinking green beer at the St Patrick's day street party in Boston until I messed up so badly I had to leave the US. I was offered a job in a tiny village in Ireland that no one's ever heard of. And I think that was the point in sending me there. How much trouble could a divorced, middle-aged witch get into in a village that boasted very few residents, one crumbling castle that attracted no tourists, and a post office that was only open Mondays and Thursdays?

You'd be surprised.

You will fall in love with this series about second chances, magical mayhem, and book club unlike any other. From the author of the best-selling *Vampire Knitting Club* series.

You can get Rafe's origin story for free when you join Nancy's no-spam newsletter at NancyWarrenAuthor.com.

Come join Nancy in her private Facebook group where we talk about books, knitting, pets and life.

www.facebook.com/groups/NancyWarrenKnitwits

THE VAMPIRE BOOK CLUB

CHAPTER 1

Have you ever wondered what your life would be like if you'd made one crucial decision differently? What if you hadn't married that man that everyone said was perfect? If you'd taken the job you wanted instead of that one with the good medical benefits? What if you'd moved to New York after college instead of Seattle?

I used to imagine what would have happened if I'd taken the other path. Maybe not the road less traveled, just not traveled by me. It was a harmless exercise to pass the time while I toiled at my boring job, safe from any threat of change.

Until one day I messed with fate.

And I was punished.

I got change all right. More than I could have imagined. My staid life was uprooted. My road was forked. Frankly, I was forked.

At forty-five, I was both divorced and widowed (from the same man), I lost the secure but dull job I'd had for ten years, and the powers that be sent me across the sea to Ireland.

It all happened so fast, my head was still spinning when

my Aer Lingus flight from Seattle landed in Dublin. From there, I took a train to Cork. It was early May, and as I looked out the window, I began to realize why they called Ireland the Emerald Isle. It was so vibrantly green, and between fields of cows and sheep, ruined castles and cottages, we stopped at pretty-sounding towns and cities to let passengers on and off. I smiled when we passed through Limerick and started making up rhymes in my head. They weren't very good, but they passed the time.

There once was a misguided witch
Who tried a man's fate to switch
Her punishment set
To Ireland she must get
But better than feathers and pitch!

From Cork city, I got a bus, though I vowed to come back and explore the pretty city when I was settled. Finally, jet-lagged and travel-weary, I arrived in my new home. The town of Ballydehag.

The bus let me off in front of Finnegan's Grocery. As the curly-haired driver retrieved my two heavy suitcases from the storage compartment underneath the bus, I thanked him. He replied, "Good luck to you, ma'am."

There's a way of wishing a person luck that sounds like you actually wish them good things, and then there's a way of wishing a person good luck that sounds more like, "What on earth have you done?"

I was wondering what on earth I'd done, too, but I was here, now. I pulled my phone out with the address of my new home and then stared vaguely about me. I had no idea where I was, except that this was clearly the main street of a pretty Irish village. The street was lined with shops. A couple of old men in caps sat outside a coffee shop regarding me. I wondered if the arrival of the bus from Cork was a big event. And didn't that say a lot about how exciting this town was?

I couldn't think of anything else to do but go into Finnegan's and hope whoever worked there might know Rose Cottage.

I didn't think my suitcases would even fit through the narrow front door of the shop, and besides, this didn't look like much of a high-crime area, so I pushed my two cases up against the white plaster wall and walked in.

It was like stepping into the past. Narrow rows with shelves of groceries stretched from ceiling to floor and seemed to contain everything from eggs to pest-control products.

I heard voices and turned to the right and the only check-out. A plump woman with curly gray hair stood behind the counter. She wore a green cardigan with the sleeves rolled up past her wrists and all the mother-of-pearl buttons done up. The edge of the sweater was scalloped, and the collar of a crisp, white blouse framed her face. She was gossiping with two customers who stood on the opposite side of the counter. "Hello?" I interrupted.

The three stopped talking and all turned to stare at me. I smiled brightly and tried to look nonthreatening. "I'm wondering if you can help me. Do you have the number of a taxi?"

They all looked at each other as though they had never heard the word taxi before. "A taxicab?" I tried again. "I'm trying to get to a place called Rose Cottage. Do you know where that is?"

The man, tall and thin with pale blue eyes, looked as though a great puzzle had been solved. "Rose Cottage. Ah." He nodded. The other two nodded as well.

There was silence. Me again? "Could you direct me to Rose Cottage? I have two suitcases outside. I was hoping to get a cab to take me there."

The man scratched his head. "I could fetch me wheelbarrow."

The woman behind the counter shook her head at him. "A wheelbarrow. Honestly. I can drive you around, love. It's not far. Danny, you come and stand behind this counter, and if anyone wants to buy anything, you just write down what it is, or they can wait until I get back. I won't be a minute."

Was this woman actually going to leave her post to drive a complete stranger? "I don't want to take you away from your work," I stammered.

"Oh, it's no trouble. And you've chosen a good time. We're not very busy."

Danny looked quite pleased to walk behind the counter and stand there very importantly. He began tidying up open packs of chocolate bars as though he owned the place.

"I'm Kathleen McGinnis," said the woman who'd come from behind the cash desk. I warmed to her immediately, but I'd warm to anyone who was willing to drive me to my new home. "And you must be Quinn Callahan."

I did a double take. "You knew I was coming?"

"I've been on the lookout for you." Her Irish accent was still a novelty to me, and I could have listened to her the way I'd listen to a bedtime story. And the way I was going, with jet lag and all that had gone before, I'd be asleep before we reached Rose Cottage.

We came out of the shop onto the sidewalk, and Kathleen McGinnis took one of my heavy suitcases while I took the other. We rattled and rolled the cases up and around the corner to where a small white van was parked with Finnegan's on the side of it. She opened the double doors at the back of the van, and we hefted my suitcases inside. I nearly bumped into her as we both walked to the driver's side door, then realizing my mistake, I walked around the front of the van and got in beside her. I wasn't used to this driving on the left-hand side of the road thing and cringed as she pulled out onto the main road, not that I needed to worry. There was zero traffic.

When they had told me I was moving to a village, I don't know what I'd expected, but I'd imagined a bit more life than this. We drove down the main road and turned right and then left, and I could see the sea spreading out in front of me. In less than five minutes, she was pulling up in front of a cottage that made me cry out with pleasure. If someone had said to me, "Picture a storybook Irish cottage," Rose Cottage was exactly what I would've come up with. To start with, it was well named. The walls were white plaster, but there were climbing roses all over the front of the cottage beginning to bud. "The cottage is named for the roses, of course, and they are a sight. In a month or two, there'll be red and white and pink roses, an absolute picture. And the scent of them is heaven."

There were stone tubs in front of the front door, empty now, but I could already see them blooming with whatever I could find around here to plant in them. It was surrounded by lawn of that wonderful green color that they only seem to have in Ireland, and there was a wishing well out front. For the first time since I'd left the States, I felt there was a possibility I might one day be happy again. "This is so beautiful."

"I'm glad you like it. We hope you'll be happy here." I hadn't missed the word We. I suspected that Kathleen McGinnis was more than a shopkeeper. "I'll just show you around, let you know how things work, and then I'll have to get back to my shop."

I completely understood she'd be abandoning me very soon. That was fine. What I really needed was a nap. The way I felt now, I wouldn't wake up for days.

We pulled my cases out of the back and dragged them up the prettiest winding stone path to the front door. It was oak and solid, and the doorknocker was a Celtic knot. She took out a set of keys, disappointingly modern, and opened the front door. She stood back so that I could go in ahead of her. I wished silently that it would be as pretty inside as it was out and then dragged my case across the threshold. I walked into a square entrance way with hexagonal red tiles on the floor, hooks for hanging coats and a pine chest. From there, I walked into a beautiful, comfortable-looking front room. Two blue sofas with cushions and woolen throws flanked an old stone fireplace already set with the wood for a fire. The carved wooden mantel was lined with candlesticks each holding a fresh golden beeswax candle. Bookcases were crammed with titles I couldn't wait to get my hands on. However, the best feature of the room was the windows looking out on the craggy coastline and the ocean. I went to the window and looked out. This part of the coastline was nearly deserted but for a castle standing proud but very lonely on a promontory set back from the water. I could imagine that back in the day, it had been an excellent spot to watch out for enemies. But now it just looked lonely. The gray stone was relieved by green ivy covering the inland side of it.

"Kitchen's through here," said Kathleen, dragging me away from my reverie. I followed her voice across the hall and into a kitchen that wasn't large but was clearly the center of this house. The floor was flagstone, and the wooden cupboards had been painted a cheerful shade of blue. Inside a nook that had once been a huge fireplace was a stove that filled me with dread. "What is that?"

"Have you never seen an Aga?"

"No. Is it electric?"

She laughed at me. "It takes some getting used to, but you'll grow to love it." She explained how one stoked it for the day. The stove would keep my cottage warm. I wasn't too keen about this stoking business. Was I going to be chopping wood? I wondered if I'd have to walk to the village pump and get my day's water. Not for the first time, I wondered what I had done. But then, what choice had I had?

There was a small fridge that looked familiar and modern enough that I thought I could manage it. A farmhouse sink sat under a pretty window. No sign of a dishwasher. Kathleen opened the fridge, beckoning inside. "I stocked it with a few basics. There's milk and bread and cheese and eggs and so on." And then she moved to one of the cupboards and opened that. "And here's tea and coffee and some biscuits. Just a few things to get you started, my dear. In the fridge, you'll also find a pot of my own mulligatawny soup, in case you don't feel like coming out this evening. You may just like to get settled. Of course, if you want some company or something else to eat, there's always the pub, O'Brien's. Or The Painted Beagle—that's a bistro that serves food all day. Otherwise, there's just a coffee shop."

On the scrubbed pine kitchen table was a ceramic jug, filled with wilted flowers. She *tsked* with annoyance. "I knew I forgot something. I meant to freshen the flowers." She mumbled something that sounded like "*floridium ad vivum*" and waved her hand over the vase, and the flowers jumped to attention and perfect freshness. "That's better."

"So you are a witch. I wondered."

She chuckled. "I am at that, and I'll help you get settled and such."

She came and put her hand on my shoulder. It was a comforting gesture. "Why don't I make you a cup of tea, my dear? You look dead on your feet. Go and sit in the lounge, and I'll bring it through."

I knew I should let her get back to her shop, but the truth was, I didn't want to be alone right now. I said tea would be nice and, instead of going into the living room, I watched her. I thought I'd better get a handle on how to do things here. It didn't look that complicated to make tea. She took a perfectly normal electric kettle and plugged it in. From one of the cupboards, she fetched a blue ceramic teapot and two mismatched china mugs. Whoever had lived here before me had obviously loved flowers. They were covered in flowers, one in roses and one in what looked like pansies and daffodils. Kathleen opened a packet of shortbread biscuits and settled them on a blue china plate and, by opening several cupboards, even found a tray. I didn't talk much, just watched her efficient movements, and then when she was done we took the whole thing through to the living room. I settled into the surprisingly comfy couch, and she sat beside me and placed the tray on a slightly beaten-up but charming wooden table.

She poured the tea. I couldn't stop looking out the window at that beautiful view.

I didn't know how to start, so finally, I said, "Was this hers? The woman I'm replacing?"

Kathleen's eyes were green and knowing. She smiled slightly. "You feel it, don't you? Yes. Lucinda made this cottage her home. She still owns it and the bookshop where you'll be working. It's exactly as she left it, fully stocked, and she's left instructions for how to order new books and, well, everything you need to know."

I was walking straight out of my life and into another woman's. Strange didn't begin to describe how that felt. I'd never even met this Lucinda. "I wish I could talk to her."

Kathleen shook her head *no.* It was the answer I'd expected, but it made me uncomfortable. "I don't see what harm it can do. I only want to find out more about her business and how to run it. It's a terrible responsibility to run someone else's store, and I don't want to screw up." Totally reasonable.

"Speaking to Lucinda is forbidden, as I believe you've been informed."

"Can you even tell me where she's gone?"

"Somewhere in England. That's all I know."

"Is that what you do then? Play musical chairs with witches who haven't followed the rules?"

Her soft eyes grew suddenly hard. "What you did was a terrible crime, Quinn. And you know it. We witches may not interfere against death."

CHAPTER 2

I closed my eyes against a wash of pain. "I know. But he was dying. I only wanted to save him." I put my cup back down on the table since my hands were starting to shake. "He was my husband."

"He hadn't been your husband for years, now had he?"

The witch gossip network was efficient. This woman obviously knew all about me. "No. But he was my best friend."

"Didn't he betray you with another woman?"

The laugh I gave was more surprised than amused. "With my other best friend." What a long time ago that seemed now. "They felt terrible, I felt terrible, and for a couple of years I was miserable. We divorced and I was angry and so hurt. But, then Hannah came along and they asked me to be godmother. We made our peace. Slowly, and painfully, but in the end I saw that I'd brought two people together who were meant to be. And Greg and I were meant to be dear friends. They were my family and I didn't want to see him die like that if I could help it."

Cancer had grabbed hold of my robust former husband,

and when his daughters—who were the daughters of my heart—begged me to use my powers to save him, I'd done what I knew was wrong. I'd foolishly believed no one would ever find out.

"It's like the flapping of that butterfly's wing," she said sternly. "You change fate in one place, and you don't know what reaction you've caused somewhere else. What you did could have had terrible consequences."

Worse, it was all for nothing. "But he died anyway."

"It doesn't matter. He didn't die when he was meant to. You interfered. We don't know yet what effect that may have had."

I was convinced there hadn't been any. How could one unimportant man, unimportant to most of the world but very important to me and to his current wife and their children, how could that have hurt the great universe? I'd used all my magic, all the herbs I knew and all the healthy remedies, and still he'd faded away. So in the end, I had done what I knew I should not. I'd used a spell so powerful that it could prevent death. And it had, for about two months. My ex-husband had seemed to be in remission. He gained back some weight, began to laugh again and talk about the future. And then one night, he died in his sleep. Even so, by prolonging his life, I'd broken a sacred rule. Now I was being punished.

"But why did they send me here?" Kathleen at least would speak to me. My own sisters in Seattle had pretty much shunned me. I thought that would be my punishment until I was sent here. One of my former witch sisters and someone I'd considered a close friend had come by with an airline ticket and address and instructions on how to get here. They'd given me two weeks to wrap up my entire life. And the sad thing was, at the age of forty-five, how easily I'd been able to do that. I'd never had children of my own or a long-term relationship after the marriage failed.

I'd rented out my little house, easy to do in thriving Seattle. I'd worked as a librarian in a law firm, and when I gave my two weeks' notice, no one seemed too devastated to see me go. I'd always been a little different, never entirely fit in. And now here I was in middle age, starting over like I was twenty-something. Only I had a lot less naïve optimism than I'd had in my twenties. And a lot more baggage.

Here I was, running a bookstore for a modest wage and renting this lovely cottage for a modest sum. If that was a punishment, I supposed there were worse ones. And at least now I knew there was at least one witch in the area.

That castle kept drawing my eye. Finally, I asked, "Is it a ruin? That castle?"

She glanced out too at the formidable castle. "They call that the Devil's Keep."

"Bet that really brings in the tourists."

She shook her head. "No tourists. It's owned privately by a man named Lochlan Balfour. He's very rich and very private and also very generous. He's a great benefactor in this area. He made his fortune in some kind of tech startup that I don't remotely understand. We see him in the village once in a while. He's always pleasant, but he spends most of his time in the castle, where he runs his company, and he travels a lot. Mainly it's his housekeeper, Dolores Tierney, who comes to the village to pick up the mail and get the groceries and such. I believe he entertains quite a bit. They often seem to have house parties."

"Is he single?" She'd spoken of him in the singular.

Her gaze was sharp. "He is, but don't you go getting any ideas."

My eyebrows went up at that. "You think I'm looking for a boyfriend?" She could not have been more wrong. "Our... calling doesn't make dating or marriage easy." I'd met Greg right after college in the law firm where I was a librarian. He was a lawyer. And for a while I believed I could live a very normal life in mainstream society. But the truth was, mainstream society didn't fit me any better than the business suits and heels I'd forced myself to wear to the office.

The divorce had forced me to finally be myself. I'd still worn suits and heels to the office, but in my own time, I wore colorful clothes that made me happy. Crystal necklaces and shoes that were comfortable to walk in. My nails were short, and there were often green stains on my skin from working in the garden with my herbs. Still, divorce had taken away my appetite for romance and, while I'd had relationships in the last fifteen years, none had stuck.

"I know what you mean. I married, all right, but I kept my skills a secret. When Barry died, a part of me finally got to live."

"Sometimes it sucks being a witch."

She leaned over and patted my knee. "You'll find your way. I'll do everything I can to help you. Just do your best to fit in, and don't do anything foolish."

I didn't know how much power she had. "Am I allowed to use my magic at all?"

She laughed at that. Her laugh was musical and light. "You're a witch. Of course you must use your powers. But you must follow the rules."

I felt like there was an implied *or else,* but I didn't push to discover what that might be. Banishment to this tiny village in the middle of nowhere seemed about as much as I could take.

"When do I start work?"

"That's up to you. Get yourself settled in, then go and have a look at your shop. That's the key for the front door there." She pointed to a key ring that was attached to the key ring from my house. "It's called The Blarney Tome, and it's the only bookstore on the high street. You won't be able to miss it."

"The Blarney Tome?" Seriously?

"It was Lucinda's little joke. We're not far from Blarney Castle and the famous stone, you see. And I suppose she liked the play on words."

We'd both finished our tea by now, and I stifled a huge yawn. She rose. "I'll leave you to settle in. I must get back to the shop before that foolish man makes a mess of things. I've written my phone number down and put it in the kitchen. You may call me anytime, or drop by if you're puzzled by anything." She smiled again. "This won't be easy, but you'll manage it. You have a good face. Trustworthy eyes. I believe you'll be very happy here."

But for how long? I didn't even know how long my banishment would last. Or did they plan to leave me here forever? She'd made it sound as though I had some choice in this matter, but we both knew I didn't.

After she left, I humped my cases up the stairs. There were two bedrooms up here and the cottage's only bathroom. I peeked into both rooms and immediately settled on the larger one. It was obviously the master. It had a sloping roof line, and the windows looked out to the sea. There were

French doors that opened onto a little balcony where I could imagine myself sitting and drinking my coffee in the mornings. Maybe sketching or reading.

I would find my way. I would have to. And the nice thing about being far away from a big city like Seattle was that I couldn't get into any trouble. Not here in this backwater. It must be a great relief to my sister witches, and it was oddly a relief to me too. It would be very easy to resist temptation when I wasn't offered any.

The bed was freshly made with gorgeous Irish linens. The duvet was a creamy white, covered with patterns of green shamrocks. It made me smile. I'd feel lucky every time I got in or out of that bed. And I could certainly use some luck. A dressing table, painted white, with an old silver-plated comb, brush and mirror set decorating its top and a triple mirror sat in an alcove. A wardrobe, also white, took up another wall. The floors were wood plank, with a soft rug that surrounded the bed.

The second bedroom was smaller and contained a single bed and a small desk. Office and guest room—if I ever had any guests. I pushed back the curtains to check out the view from this side, and as I did, I noticed paw prints on the windowsill. I ran my finger over them lightly. A cat had lived here.

I continued my tour. The bathroom had a nice, big, deep tub with a shower fixed over it. It looked a bit old-fashioned, but I'd manage. I ran water in the sink, washed my face and brushed my teeth and then stripped down to my underwear. I crawled into that bed and snuggled into its beautiful softness.

As I drifted to sleep, I thought I heard a cat meowing.

CHAPTER 3

I woke and stretched my arms and legs out in the comfortable bed, feeling better than I had for a long time. I opened my eyes. Of course I hadn't bothered to close the curtains. I'd pretty much just passed out on the bed. As I got out of bed and padded to the window, I saw the gray light like pewter on the choppy waves, and I had the oddest impression that instead of protecting the land from the sea, that strange, lonely castle was protecting the sea from the land. It was foolish and whimsical. I'd been in Ireland less than a day, and already I was full of whimsy and strange tales.

I had no idea what time it was. I was so jet-lagged. I looked at my mobile phone and discovered it was seven at night. I entered the bathroom and climbed into the big, old bathtub. For all its antiquity, the shower was actually pretty good. Nice, strong flow from the shower head. When I got out, I felt much better, refreshed, and maybe I'd washed some of my sadness down that Irish drain. I hoped so. I didn't want to be sad anymore.

As Kathleen had reminded me earlier, Greg and I hadn't

been married when he died. And yet, because he'd been a close friend and such an important part of my life, a part of me died when he went. I missed Emily, Greg's current wife—well, his widow now. And I missed his two teenaged daughters.

I'd lost my mother to cancer when I was eighteen. I remembered begging her to use her witchcraft to save herself, for my powers came through her. She'd taken my hand in her frail ones and told me that fate was more powerful than any witch.

I should have listened, but when Greg's daughters, Hannah and Ashley, had begged me to help him, I'd been transported back to the misery of losing my mom. I'd interfered. But as usual, my mom had been right. Fate was a tough opponent, and she did not appreciate being messed with.

I ate the mulligatawny soup with the fresh bread that tasted homemade and had been left in my bread bin. I washed it all down with another cup of Irish tea, tidied up all my dishes, and it was still only eight at night. I was wide awake, full of the kind of restless energy that you get when you've been cooped up on a plane, a train and a bus for much too long. I needed to get out. I couldn't quite handle the little car that was parked around behind my cottage and, apparently, came with the place. But there was a bike. I wasn't suicidal, so I made sure that there was a working headlight, and I decided to take a little trip into town. I dried my hair, put on light makeup just in case, threw on a warm sweater and light jacket over my jeans and pushed off.

I would never win any biking race, but then, neither would this bike. It was a little old, a little creaky, and instead of twenty-one sleek gears, it had a basket attached to its front.

This was a bicycle for exploring country roads and picking up baguettes and a few items from the grocery store. If I were a bike, I would be this one.

In perfect accord, we cruised our way back toward the high street of this tiny town. Even in this remote part of Ireland, my maps app still worked. I figured it had taken about five minutes to drive here and it was maybe eight on the bicycle to get back again. I pedaled past the grocery store, closed now. Across from it was a pharmacy. There was the coffee shop, and as I rode along, I recognized the bookstore right away. It was the bookshop equivalent of my old and perfectly darling bicycle.

This wasn't like any bookstore I'd ever seen before. You weren't going to find thousands of the latest titles, and there'd be no coffee shop inside. This was a bookshop out of an Irish novel. The woodwork surrounding the square front window was painted blue (I was getting the feeling that blue was Lucinda's color). Sure enough, above the glass door was a sign: The Blarney Tome. Thanks to a streetlight, I could see that the front window display was a collection of titles by Irish authors. There was Maeve Binchy and James Joyce, John Banville and his crime-writing alter ego, Benjamin Black. This was the kind of bookshop I always wandered into when I was on holiday and exploring a new town. I'd only planned to ride by the bookshop, but I had the keys in my pocket. Why not?

With an odd sense of anticipation, knowing this would be my life for the near future, I took out the keys. I pushed the first one into the lock on the front door, but it was the wrong key. After idly wondering how many keys a tiny bookshop like this would need, I tried the second key, and the door obligingly opened. Before I stepped across the threshold, I flapped my hand against the side of the wall inside the door until I found a triple light switch. I flipped all the switches.

The shop immediately sprang to life. Again, it was almost more like my fantasy of a bookshop than the real thing. Floor-to-ceiling shelves stocked books, and I could see that not all of them were new. There were so many books you could lose an elephant in here and not notice.

There were little reading areas with comfy chairs. A cash desk was old and beaten up and featured not a fancy computer but a real old-fashioned cash register. I couldn't help myself. I decided to go and push that register so it would cough out its cash drawer.

As I stepped in, I noticed the scattered mail on the floor. I picked it up. It was all addressed to Lucinda Corrigan, my predecessor and the owner of this lovely little bookstore. Idly, I wondered if she'd consider selling it to me if I decided to stay. If I sold my Seattle house and paid off the mortgage I'd have a tidy sum left over. It wasn't a fortune but in a little town like this? I bet I could afford a shop and probably a decent down payment on my little cottage. I couldn't believe it. One nap in the comfortable bed, and I already thought of it as mine.

I walked deeper into the shop and fell even more under its charm. The floors were wide plank, and I bet they were original. They were dark with age, and there were dings and scratches to give them character and rugs scattered across their surface. Not fancy thick rugs but threadbare, cheerful rugs that begged to be walked on and didn't mind if an animal or a child sat or played on them. The easy chairs looked like they had come from thrift stores, or maybe they got donated by the people who lived in the area. They were as mismatched as the china in my kitchen and just as charming, begging a person to curl up in their depths with a good book. I felt, I don't know, contentment, I think.

I stood there and listened and let the feelings come to me. You don't have to be a witch to appreciate that homes and houses and even stores hold history and emotions. Lucinda had created a welcoming, contented space, and I could feel how much that had come back to her from her happy customers. I could almost hear children's voices searching for the next Harry Potter. I imagined people searching out stories their hearts desired and Lucinda doing her best to find them.

As I breathed in the scents of old leather and paper and a hint of lemon furniture polish, I became aware of another scent. It was like a bitter fog that had crept in behind me. I glanced around, my heart picking up speed. How foolish. I hadn't even closed the door. It stood wide as though I were open for business. Luckily, there was nobody on the street, so I wasn't about to be mobbed by book-starved bibliophiles. Okay, I'd had my peek inside. I'd get out and come back tomorrow when it was daylight. But for good luck, I was determined to bang open that cash drawer. I bet there was a lucky penny inside it for me. That seemed like the kind of thing Lucinda might do.

I walked over and stepped behind the cash desk, where I would soon be making change. In euros. The unpleasant scent grew stronger. It had a tang and a bitterness to it. Almost like—

Blood.

I looked down. There was a man lying there on the floor behind the desk, facedown. All I could see was a balding head and some gray hair. He was slightly portly and wearing a pale blue jacket over worn jeans. On his feet were old sneakers.

I'd never seen unnatural death before, but it didn't take a genius to work out that this guy hadn't died of old age. Blood pooled from beneath him. It was very dark. I couldn't touch him. I wanted to, but I couldn't. Anyway, if there's one thing being a witch is good for, it's being able to tell that someone's dead without actually having to poke your fingers on their dead flesh. This guy's spirit was gone.

The man on the floor was dead.

CHAPTER 4

So far, I hadn't made so much as a peep. I was frozen in shock. There must be things I had to do. Call 911. I pulled out my mobile. My hands were shaking. No, not 911. Not in Ireland. Nine something. Was it 999? I hit the first nine and then I heard a noise at the front door. I glanced up and there was a man standing there. A tall, mysterious stranger.

My composure instantly left me. I screamed.

Had the murderer come back? Was he going to kill me? No one even knew I was here except Kathleen McGinnis.

He stepped closer. I screamed again. My hands were shaking too badly to manage 999. I didn't even know what I was doing. I flattened my back against the wall and screamed again.

The man stopped moving. He looked as though the noise was hurting his ears. Good, then he could just get out. "I'm not here to hurt you," he said calmly.

Ha, if there was ever a man who looked like he could hurt you, it was this one. He was tall. He had to be six foot three. Broad of shoulder, thick with muscle. He had blond hair and the coldest ice-blue eyes I'd ever seen. His face was pale and chiseled. The blade of his nose was long and straight. He had a strong jaw with the most ludicrously out-of-place dimple in it. It was the only softness I could see. He stood tall and as unyielding as that castle near my cottage.

I stopped screaming, but I wasn't feeling any more relaxed. "Who are you?" My voice came out like a pathetic wimpy croak. I was annoyed with myself. I was a grown woman. I was a witch. If my head was working right, I could probably think up some spell to repel him. Of course my head wasn't working at all. I felt fuddled and frightened and jet-lagged, and I wished I was back in my bed in Seattle.

He held his hands out, loose and relaxed, I suppose so I could see he didn't hold a weapon. They were nice hands. Well-made and long-fingered. More artistic than deadly. Finally, he answered my question. "I'm Lochlan Balfour."

My ears perked up at that. I knew only two people here in this village. One was Kathleen McGinnis. The other, and only because she'd mentioned his name, was Lochlan Balfour. I looked at him. "You own the castle beside my cottage?"

An emotion crossed the cold ice of his eyes. Like a flicker of light. Could it be amusement? "I do. I was passing, and I saw the door standing open. Is everything all right?"

I saw his nostrils twitch, and I had the strangest sensation that he knew as well as I did that all was not well. I shook my head. "There's a man on the ground." I wanted to glance down again at the corpse at my feet, but I didn't dare take my eyes off this frightening-looking stranger. "He's—"

"Dead."

I knew it. He'd been able to sense the death just the way I had. Was he a witch? He didn't look like one, and wouldn't

Kathleen McGinnis have mentioned it if I had a witch for a neighbor? He paused for a moment while all these thoughts tumbled in my head like a faulty dryer. "May I come closer?"

"Why?" I was frantically trying to think up protection spells, but my mind remained stubbornly blank.

"I live locally. I might be able to recognize him."

I noticed that he hadn't said anything about seeing if he was still alive or calling an ambulance. Still, I nodded. The sooner we got on with this, the sooner I could get out of here. Preferably on a plane back home.

He must have seen how freaked I was, for instead of coming around my side of the cash desk, he very carefully made his way around the other way, his gaze never leaving mine. I began to relax a little as he moved away from the door and I had a clear path out onto the street. It didn't take much time with those long legs to get around the back of the cash desk. Before he did anything, he gazed down at the dead man. Then he dropped to his knees. Instead of feeling for a pulse, he did a very odd thing. He leaned forward and sniffed. Like a wolf scenting the air for prey.

He glanced at me watching him and, almost as an afterthought, picked up the man's wrist in his. He quickly put it down again. "He's dead."

"I was about to call 999," I said.

For the first time, he smiled, and it was no surprise to discover that he had beautiful white teeth. He was the most gorgeous scary dude I'd ever seen. I thought he might be around my age. Maybe a little younger. I had a fleeting image of us on a first date. What I'd discovered with internet dating at my age was that we all had so much baggage, we needed a second plane just to haul it around. Something about this guy told me he had plenty of baggage of his own. Still, he was very nice to look at, and he did take my mind momentarily off the horror of the dead guy in my shop.

Lucinda's shop, I reminded myself, but of course, Lucinda wasn't here. I was.

"We're a bit remote out here. It'll be some time before the Gardaí can get here."

"Gardaí?"

"An Garda Síochána. The Irish police."

"Oh." Good to know. So in emergencies the Irish phoned a different number, they called their police a weird name, and they drove on the wrong side of the road. Oh, and their currency was the euro. I was going to fit right in. Then I processed what he'd said. "How long will it take them? I don't want to hang around all night with a dead man."

"No. That's rather disturbing. We should call Dr. Milsom."

Okay, I'd bite. "Who's he?"

With my luck, he'd have a PhD in music theory.

"Andrew Milsom is the village doctor. Since we don't have anyone else, he's also the pathologist and the coroner. And the only morgue is in his surgery."

"Kind of a one-stop death shop?" I asked.

His lips twitched. "Something like that."

We looked at each other. I held out my phone, empty of any contacts in the area except for Kathleen McGinnis. "Do you have his number?"

Before he could answer, Kathleen McGinnis herself came rushing in the front door. Almost as though I'd summoned her. Maybe I had. She glanced between us, a concerned look on her face. "I heard screaming. Quinn, what are you doing here? And Lochlan."

He looked at me as if to say, "Over to you."

"I had a nap this afternoon and then I woke up not tired. Your soup was excellent, by the way." *Oh, shut up.* Nerves and stress and shock were making me babble. "Anyway, I thought I'd just come into town and look around. Then when I got here, I decided to come in and see the bookstore for myself."

Heaven knows how long I would have kept babbling had Lochlan not taken control of the conversation. "There's a dead man behind the cash desk."

Yep. That pretty much summed up where I was going in my rambling way.

Kathleen looked horrified. "Dead?"

"As a doornail."

"But who is it?" she asked. Did she think I knew? I shrugged and looked at Lochlan. He kept the shrug going and passed it back to her. She came around my side of the desk and looked down. "Oh, dear," she said. "It's Declan O'Connor."

No. Is it? "And who is Declan O'Connor?" I asked her.

She pinched her lips together and shook her head. "Poor Eileen."

Not exactly the answer I'd been looking for, but I appreciated that shock had snuck up on her too. "I understand emergency services are far away?" And let that not be true.

She leaned against the old wooden cash desk, her gaze still on the dead man. "It'll take at least an hour for anyone to get here. We should call the doctor."

Okay, at least she was agreeing with my blond friend over there. She looked at both of us. "Has anyone called him?"

Again, I held out my phone, full of contacts in Seattle that weren't going to do us much good here. Lochlan merely stared back at her. She nodded. “Right.” She pulled out her own mobile, scrolled through her contacts and made the call.

This was such a nightmare. She told Dr. Milsom that there’d been a suspicious death and could he please come to the bookshop. I didn’t hear what he said, but when she hung up, she assured us that he was on his way and that he’d call the Gardaí himself.

It felt strange calling a country doctor to a murder scene. How was that his job? But then, how busy could his practice be out here? Apart from the odd stab wound from locals picking shamrocks, did anything ever go wrong in this picture-postcard of a town? Then I glanced down and revised that opinion.

“Well,” Kathleen said. “This has been very unpleasant for you, Quinn. And on your first day, too. You should have waited till tomorrow to come and look at your shop. Whatever were you thinking?” Like it was my fault a guy was dead in my bookstore.

Then she turned to Lochlan. “And it’s a very odd time to be out shopping for books now, isn’t it?”

He glanced at me and then at the door. “I wasn’t. I was on my way to the pub, if you must know. I walked by and the door was wide open. Then this woman began screaming. What would you have had me do?”

She smoothed down her feathers. “Well, I appreciate the gentlemanly concern. But we’re all right now. You can go.”

I felt that he wanted to, but he shook his head. “I’ll wait until the doctor gets here, just to back up this young lady’s story.” *Young lady?* Seriously? Still, I kind of liked that he’d called me that. Then I got to the substance of his remark and felt as though the floor were tilting beneath me. A guy dead on the floor? Me new in town? And I'd stumbled across him? Who was the most likely suspect?

Unaware that I'd written an entire murder mystery in my head where I was the unfairly accused killer, Kathleen smiled at him. "That's good of you. Have you met, then?"

"Not exactly," I said.

"Quinn Callahan is new in town. She just arrived today, in fact. She's taking over the bookshop."

"Welcome to Ballydehag," Lochlan said.

Was he being sarcastic? Hard to tell. "Thank you."

"And this is Lochlan Balfour. He lives in the castle and is a great benefactor of our village."

I hated the way she was sucking up to him. If he was as rich as she said he was, throwing a few euros around this little village was probably like me putting a dollar in the charity box at the grocery store at home.

We stood around in uncomfortable silence. It was hard to have any kind of a conversation when there was a dead man at our feet. A veritable elephant in the room if there ever was one. Also, now that the shock was starting to wear off, the enormity of this horror was gaining on me. What had I walked into?

I wanted to—well, there were a lot of things I wanted to do, and none of them involved standing here. Still, only about ten minutes passed before another man walked through that door. He looked to be around fifty, with dark hair lightly threaded with gray and dark brown eyes. He had a couple of extra pounds on him and a cynical, world-weary look about him. Since he carried a medical bag, I had to assume this was the doctor.

What made a doctor come to a place like this? Had he

killed somebody by accident? Were there lawsuits pending against him? He looked like he hadn't been sleeping well. But at least he had his bag with him. Kathleen said, "Over here," and pointed behind the cash desk.

He glanced at me and nodded, and I moved away. He came around and stood looking down at the dead man. Then, to my surprise, the first thing he did was pull out a camera and take a couple of photographs. "Shouldn't you check that he's dead?" I asked. I'd seen plenty of cop shows in my time. They didn't grab their cameras the second they entered a crime scene.

He looked at me like I wasn't the sharpest scalpel in his toolkit. "Oh, he's dead." He took another photograph. "Question is, how long has he been so?"

This guy seemed to have his professions mixed up. He was acting like a cop. But then, I supposed, in a town this size, coroner equaled cop, at least until the real cops showed up. Finally, he put on a pair of surgical gloves, then he walked around to the guy's head, squatted down and felt for a carotid artery. He even touched his hand to the blood. Ew.

From his crouched position, he glanced up at us. "I take it Declan O'Connor finally got what he deserved," he said.

CHAPTER 5

"No one deserves that," Kathleen said as the doctor returned for his bag. I didn't know what Declan O'Connor had done, but I had to agree with her.

Dr. Milsom said, "I can take it from here. Why don't you go back to whatever you were doing? The Guards will want to talk to you when they get here, so don't go far."

"You mean, I suppose, that we're in your way?" Kathleen asked, rather sharply.

"Very much, yes." He was English, I realized. Not Irish. And manners weren't his strong suit.

Kathleen looked like she might argue with him, but I was very happy to take myself elsewhere. I hadn't even started work yet, and there was a man lying dead in my shop. I didn't want to be too ghoulish, but I wondered if I'd ever get the blood out of the floor. Poor Lucinda, did she even have insurance for something like that?

I was, however, responsible, I supposed. I hesitated. "Do you need me to come back and lock up when you're...um, when you're done?"

"No. Don't come back in until the Gardaí tell you to. This is a possible crime scene."

"Possible crime scene?" Did this guy get his medical degree off the Internet? "He's lying in a pool of blood."

The doctor's face was a study in irritation when he glanced at me. He pointed to a smudgy, sticky mark on the corner of the desk that I hadn't noticed. "He hit his head there, on the way down. Could have broken his nose when he hit the floor. That could account for the blood." Okay, so he was more observant than he looked.

"So you don't think he was murdered?" Well, that was good news at least.

For one second.

"I do think he was murdered. But we'll need to investigate to be certain."

"Come along, then, Quinn," Kathleen said, suddenly taking my arm and urging me toward the door. "Let's let Dr. Milsom do his work."

On the wall beside the door was a community bulletin board, the kind where people offered pianos for sale and flats to rent. Someone advertised puppies. Right at that moment, the thought of a furry bundle of unconditional love seemed like the perfect addition to my household. I walked forward and reached for the handwritten page. Kathleen saw my intent and said, "Yer too late, lovey. Cassandra's dog had the dearest little puppies, but they were all given away, I'm afraid."

"Oh." Probably getting a puppy right now wasn't the smartest idea anyway. Especially as I didn't know if I'd be staying. I was about to turn away from the community board when a fluttering newspaper article caught my eye. The headline announced: “Best-Selling Novelist Disappears from Ship.” I managed to scan the first paragraph. “In a plot that could have come from one of his own blockbusters, suspense novelist Bartholomew Branson disappeared from *Queen of the Hebrides.* Branson was celebrity lecturer on the luxury cruise when he went missing.” The paper was dated two weeks earlier. No wonder I hadn’t seen the story. The only newspaper I’d seen in the last couple of weeks had been the stuff I was using to wrap up dishes and things that were now stowed in a storage locker.

I turned then and followed Kathleen and Lochlan. “I didn’t know Bartholomew Branson was missing,” I said as we walked out of the store. Obviously I was quite happy to take our conversation in a different direction.

Kathleen nodded. “It’s a terrible thing. He was meant to speak in Dublin to start an Ireland-wide tour. I was going myself to hear him and get his latest book signed. The tickets had sold out months before, but, of course, everything’s been canceled now.”

“But what do you think happened to him?”

“They think he fell overboard.”

I shuddered. That sounded like a very unpleasant way to end a cruise. “Could he have left at one of the stops?” I imagined being a celebrity author on a cruise might be tiring. He probably couldn’t put his nose out of his own cabin without being mobbed by fans who’d paid a lot of money to spend days at sea with him. Perhaps he snuck off at a port of call with no one being the wiser.

“Well, if he did, he hasn’t turned up. They’ve looked in all the hospitals and morgues and searched missing persons. Small boats went out looking for him, but it’s a big sea out there, and no one knows exactly where he might've gone overboard. If he even did."

"Well, it's a mystery."

We hadn't gone far when a woman came forward from the other side of the street. "Lochlan," she said. When she came into the light, I saw a woman in her thirties, smartly dressed. "There's a problem in the New York office. I think you'll want to get onto them."

He nodded, then turned to us. His smile was cool but charming. "Business calls, I'm afraid."

"Well, we know where to find you when the Gardaí get here," Kathleen said, and with a backward wave, he and the woman walked in the other direction.

"He runs a worldwide business from here?" I was astonished.

"These days, you can run them from anywhere," she reminded me.

She was right, but how many head offices had Devil's Keep on their letterhead?

CHAPTER 6

The pub was called O'Brien's, and not only was it around the corner from the bookshop, but it was adorable. Painted red, with harps and shamrocks drawn all over the side of the building, it looked like fun. There was a chalkboard outside offering Murphy's and Beamish ales and three specials for tonight's dinner: Irish stew, oysters and chips, and gammon steak.

Kathleen saw me looking and said, "Are you hungry?"

"No. Your mulligatawny soup was delicious, thank you. And that bread was amazing."

"We may be a small village, but we take our food very seriously." She paused, then sighed. "I'm not sure when you'll next get fresh bread, though. Declan O'Connor was the baker."

"Oh." I must have eaten from one of the last loaves he ever baked.

"The food at the pub is anything as good as what you'll find in Dublin, perhaps not as wide a selection, but you'll not be going hungry here. And for groceries, I pride myself on stocking most everything you need. If you've a mind to drive farther afield, there's the SuperValu about half an hour's drive away."

She smiled at me. "And, of course, if there's something you particularly fancy from the States, like, I can try and bring it in for you."

For the first time, I thought about the advantages of living in a small village. "You'd do that for me?"

"Of course I would. I bring in English sweets for Mr. Ballantine, even though you can't tell me the Butlers chocolates aren't the best in the world."

I was astonished that we were leaving the scene of death and heading straight for the pub. But what were our choices? I did not want to go home to that silent, lonely cottage all by myself. Some of Declan O'Connor's essence seemed to be clinging to me, like an odor I couldn't get out of a sweater.

Beside me, Kathleen said, "You know a good cleansing spell, I hope?"

It was funny, because that was exactly what I'd been thinking about. I'd be doing that as soon as I got home. I nodded.

"Good."

"Do you think it's a bit ghoulish of us to go to the pub? With what we know is back at the bookshop?"

She looked at me with a kind of world-weary expression. "What would you have us do? The doctor's there, and he'll do what's necessary. And then the Gardaí will take over. There's nothing you can do for the dead man. And I think you and I could both use a glass of whiskey."

Copy that.

Before we went in, I stopped her. "What did Dr. Milsom mean? About Declan O'Connor getting what he deserved?"

She hesitated, then said, "I really couldn't say."

"But the doctor seemed to know something."

"Small towns are rife with rumor, Quinn. Half of the things you hear aren't true."

But Dr. Milsom had seemed to be a man of few words. He didn't look like a gossip.

When we entered the pub, it was as though we'd entered a magical kingdom. Where the streets had been deserted, O'Brien's was full of life and music and people. There was a violinist playing Celtic music in the corner, and people were sitting in chairs in a semi-circle around her, clapping and tapping their feet in time to the merry tune.

Kathleen glanced around the room and then seemed to jump up in the air. "Jesus Mary and Joseph, that's Eileen O'Connor."

I looked at her. If Declan O'Connor was the dead man in my shop, then was it possible that Eileen O'Connor was—

"Declan's wife. Well, widow now, poor love." Kathleen turned to me. "But don't you say a word. It's not up to us to spread that news. That's for the doctor to do or, better still, the Gardaí."

I looked at the woman sitting at a corner table, laughing. She was with a much younger man and a couple enjoying a glass of beer. She looked so ordinary, so placid, so not as though her life was about to be exploded.

"Let's sit as far away from her as we can," I said in a low voice. Kathleen nodded and took two steps in the opposite direction when a loud voice called out, "Kathleen McGinnis. Come on over here and introduce us to your young friend."

Even over the sound of the Celtic fiddle, the woman's voice carried. Many heads turned to stare. I felt like the new kid in high school, walking into the cafeteria for the first time. As hard as I tried to look nonchalant, like I came in here every day, I felt measured and scrutinized. I suddenly wished I'd worn a nicer top and maybe put some earrings on.

Under her breath, Kathleen said, "There's no help for it now. Remember what I said."

Then she walked briskly ahead of me toward the very recent widow.

"Well this is a fine sight. I hope you left some whiskey for us?"

There was general laughter. I got the feeling that this pub might run out of a lot of things, but not Irish whiskey.

"This is Quinn Callahan. She'll be running the bookstore."

The woman who was Declan O'Connor's widow looked to be a pleasant sort of woman. She had curly brown hair that went to her shoulders, calm green eyes behind gold-rimmed glasses, and when she smiled, her teeth were a bit crooked. This woman had never had braces in her life. She stood and reached over the table to shake my hand. "I'm Eileen O'Connor," she said. "My husband and I run the bakery. O'Connor's Bread and Buns." She laughed and shrugged her shoulders. "Not original, I know. But we've been serving bread to the people of this town for more than twenty years."

"That's really good to know. I've heard that Irish bread is wonderful." I didn't let on that I'd already tasted some or that I doubted I'd be eating any soon.

"That it is. Our soda bread is a secret recipe that many have tried to copy. And failed. And this is my son, Liam."

The much younger man did look like her. The same curly hair, though not as long as his mother's, and the same calm green eyes. His teeth were a lot straighter though. He'd come of age more recently. He was probably twenty-five and thick-set. She said, "You'll see him in the bakery sometimes on the weekend. But he's also doing a college degree. Online. You must join us."

We glanced at each other, but what could we say? They were already shuffling closer together to make room for us. Kathleen had on a pale blue raincoat, belted at the waist. When she took it off, I saw she was wearing a blue floral dress. She must have been headed for the pub too when she walked past the bookshop. It was Saturday night. No wonder the whole village seemed to be here.

The other couple turned out to be Sean and Rosie Higgins, who were the owners of the butcher. Another husband and wife team. Sean Higgins was in his fifties with big, tattooed arms and big hands currently wrapped around a pint of Guinness. He looked as though he could butcher a huge animal without breaking a sweat. His wife was smaller and neater and no doubt ran the retail shop. I felt as though I had gone back in time. This was the kind of village where families ran businesses for years and years, probably passed them on to their sons and daughters. No doubt O'Connor's Bread and Buns would one day belong to Liam O'Connor. And he'd marry a nice local girl and continue the baking tradition. It was charming and old-fashioned, and I felt the first stirs of affection for my new home. Though they were rather overshadowed by the horror of what I'd recently discovered in my shop.

I swallowed hard. It was difficult to remain calm and friendly when I had this terrible knowledge about this woman's husband and this young man's father, and I wasn't at liberty to share.

Too much compassion, that was my failing fault. That's what my sisters told me, anyway. It was my compassion that had made me do that stupid thing in trying to save my ex-husband's life. And I felt the stirrings of it now. I wanted to take this woman's hands in my own and try and send her strength and fortitude for what was to come. Kathleen, my witch sister, must have read my thoughts, for she jabbed her foot against my ankle, and the pain drove out any thoughts of compassion.

Kathleen said, "I'll run up and get you an Irish whiskey."

I was normally a white-wine woman, but I felt that if I ever wanted to fit in here, I was going to have to at least attempt to develop a taste for Irish whiskey. So I nodded and let her go. She sent me a warning glance before she did, and I knew that I had to keep my mouth shut, whatever happened.

"Oh, it's nice to be off my feet," Eileen O'Connor said.

"Were you working today?" I imagined the shops would be open on a Saturday.

"I was, and then it was my turn to do the flowers for St. Patrick's, so it's been a long day."

A man came toward us. He was good-looking, fortyish, with twinkling gray eyes, a beard and a much younger model in tow. And I did mean model. She was stunning. In a village of ordinary-looking people, she stood out. Lustrous fair skin, the kind of lips that don't even need lipstick to draw attention to themselves. Enormous blue eyes and long blond hair. Her tight shirt and jeans showed off an impressive figure. As he drew closer, he put a casual arm around her shoulders as though he had to warn even me, another woman, that she was his prize.

"I'm guessing you must be Quinn Callahan," he said. He gave me a smile and held out his hand. While I agreed that I was in fact Quinn Callahan and returned the warm handshake, he introduced himself as Giles Murray. "I'm a photographer. My shop is down the block from yours."

I was surprised that a town this size could support a photographer. I knew so little. I imagined I had a lot to learn. My gaze went to the beautiful young woman by his side, and he said, "And this is Beatrice."

And that was it. No, this is Beatrice, my wife; Beatrice, my girlfriend; Beatrice, my long-lost daughter; my employee. Just Beatrice. She looked as though she were used to being nothing but a first name and gave me a nod and a smile. Naturally, that smile revealed the most gleaming, beautiful teeth I'd seen outside of a toothpaste commercial.

They pulled up chairs at this growing table, and then he said to Mrs. O'Connor, "And where's your man tonight?"

My heart clenched in dread. "Declan's gone to his sister's. He'll be back tomorrow or the next day. You know what she's like, ever since she lost her husband, always calling on my man to fix her dripping tap or chop her wood, mow her lawn. It's not that she can't afford to hire a handyman, but I think she wants him near her. He's family." She sounded both affectionate and irritable at the same time.

Of course, I knew that the man wasn't mowing lawns or

fixing dripping faucets. Unless he'd been moved, he was still facedown in a pool of his own blood in the bookshop.

I had to swallow down half the contents of my stomach just thinking about it. Luckily, Kathleen returned with two glasses of Irish whiskey. I was sure I'd tasted it at some point in my life and obviously hadn't liked it enough to make a habit of drinking it. Still, everyone around the table picked up their glasses and said *sláinte*. The baker's wife looked to me and added, "Welcome to Ballydehag."

CHAPTER 7

I raised my own glass and repeated the toast, and then I took a cautious sip of the Irish whiskey. It was, as I had feared, both fiery and, well, mostly just fiery. I didn't want to be a horrible cliché and cough and choke and have to be slapped on the back, so I gave my throat a minute to recover before taking a second small sip. I was never going to make a habit of drinking whiskey, but I considered it was medicinal after the shock I'd received.

Nobody seemed to notice I was struggling, thank goodness. "Do you know Lucinda well?" Giles, the photographer, asked me.

I parroted the answer that I'd been taught if this very question was asked. "No. This was arranged by an agency. Lucinda offered her cottage and bookshop, and I applied for it. Through the same agency, she found another home and job."

"What a shame you didn't get a chance to meet her. She's lovely. You'd like her." He looked puzzled and said to Kathleen, "Why did she leave? You two were always good friends. Did she tell you?"

"I think she wanted a change. I'm sure one day she'll be back."

I'd have liked to meet Lucinda, but for some reason, the sisterhood didn't want us getting together. It was weird living in someone else's house and running her bookshop when we were strangers. Though I imagined I'd get a pretty good idea of her personality just from living with her things. She hadn't cleansed her space when she left. I could feel her there. I might, one day, get around to clearing it, but it was like having the perfect roommate. She was sort of there and yet not.

"So it's just you then?"

"Yes." And didn't I sound like a real winner?

"Perhaps you should get a cat," Rosie Higgins said.

Was she being funny? I couldn't tell. Her face looked pleasant and bland, but I couldn't be certain she wasn't thinking I was heading toward crazy-cat-lady territory. Then she added, "Lucinda had a lovely one, didn't she?"

"Yes," Eileen O'Connor agreed. "Cerridwen used to sleep in the reading chairs in the bookshop. Good company, a cat. Also, keeps the mice away," said the very practical baker's wife.

It was absolutely surreal sitting here having a drink, knowing what was going on in The Blarney Tome. I couldn't take much more of this, pretending everything was fine, having a drink with a woman whose husband was dead and who didn't know it yet.

"With a name like Quinn Callahan, I'm guessing your

people hail from here," Rosie Higgins said, her voice lilting in a question. "It's an old name from around these parts."

"Honestly, I don't know. It's my father's name and he left us when I was twelve."

"Oh, I'm sorry love," Eileen O'Connor said. "Sad to lose your father so young, but he's in a better place."

No doubt by 'a better place' she meant heaven. But when I said he'd left us, I meant left us for another woman. He was the first man in my life who couldn't cope with living with a witch. Maybe he could have managed with one, but when I began to exhibit my powers it was too much for him and he left taking his work assistant with him. He used to talk about the old country, but he'd never been there either. His grandparents had come from Ireland following the great famine. I hadn't seen him since. I'd tried, when my mother was so ill to track him down, but had no luck. Brendan Callahan had disappeared. I imagined, by now, that he was dead.

Kathleen kept fidgeting beside me, and I could feel that her nerves were as jangled as mine. When her mobile buzzed, I heard it. She looked at the call display and excused herself. I knew instinctively that the call was related to Declan O'Connor's death.

Because I was watching for it, I saw her motion me over. I excused myself and hoped they'd think I was going to the ladies' room.

Kathleen pulled me aside and told me that she'd been asked to take Eileen and Liam outside, where a garda was waiting. And I was free to go home. "But don't say anything to anyone, of course. They'll want to interview you in the morning."

That felt a bit like a letdown. I'd been so edgy, ready to tell my story to some sharp-eyed detective who'd no doubt try to catch me out in a lie. Instead, I was being sent home until the morning. I supposed it made sense that the police—Gardaí—would want to focus on Declan's wife and son tonight and maybe try to find someone who held a grudge against the baker.

I'd only arrived in town earlier today, so the chances were very slim I'd be the killer or even know anything.

Dr. Milsom had suggested Declan O'Connor finally got what he deserved. What had the baker done? And who had dished out whatever the doctor thought he deserved?

RIDING my bicycle back to the cottage that night was without doubt the most terrifying eight minutes of my life. Once away from the high street, the town of Ballydehag didn't bother with streetlights. The lonely, winding country roads that had seemed so romantic on my ride in now seemed the stuff of nightmares and every slasher movie I'd ever foolishly watched.

The moon was a weak sliver behind scattered clouds. The headlight on my bike seemed like one eye gazing ahead into impenetrable darkness. I kept thinking something dark and terrifying, like a murderer maybe, was following me. I was pedaling as fast as I could, but the poor, old girl only really had one speed. A cow mooed in a field as I went by, and I nearly fell off my bike.

By the time I reached Rose Cottage, I was a wreck. I leaned the bike against the shed and pulled out the house keys. My hands were shaking. Fortunately, I'd left a light on. I walked as quickly as I could toward the lit back door that led into that cheerful kitchen. Safety beckoned, and then a dark shadow moved.

For the second time that night, I screamed. I literally thought I was going to have a heart attack, my heart was banging so hard against my ribs.

The shadow was between me and the door. I thought about turning and racing back to the bike when the shadow meowed.

A cat. Not a murderer but someone's stray pet.

"Pussycat," I said as sternly as I dared. "What are you doing here? You scared the life out of me."

I got another pitiful meow in response.

I made it to the door and opened it, and the black shadow whipped inside before I could decide whether I was going to invite the cat in or not.

I closed the door behind me and locked it and then turned on the light in the kitchen. The cat turned and stared at me. It was all black with green eyes and seemed to be expecting something from me.

"Are you lost?" I asked.

It meowed again and came close to me. It nudged its nose against my leg and then walked all around me, rubbing against my legs. I picked it up, and the cat nestled against me. It was so comforting, even for a few minutes, not to be alone.

I got milk out and poured it into a china saucer, this one decorated with lilies of the valley, and the cat was very happy to lap that up. Then it looked at me as though to say, what's next?

I opened all the cupboards and, surprisingly, found four tins of cat food. But of course, Lucinda had had a cat. I supposed wherever she'd gone, she hadn't bothered to pack the cat food along with her.

"You're in luck," I said. "I hope you like ..." I squinted at the can. "Tuna?"

The way it was purring and meowing, I didn't think Puss in Boots here was too worried about the flavor of cat food. More about the speed at which it was delivered. I fetched another saucer, faded yellow roses, and dumped the can of food onto the saucer. The cat was on its hind legs, it was so eager to get at the food. It didn't look like a stray. It looked sleek and well cared for. But when I put the food down, it attacked. I stood out of its way while it gobbled up three-quarters of the food and then, licking its whiskers, the cat looked at me as though wondering what was next on the program.

"I should probably put you out. Somebody must be waiting for you." The cat looked at me as though I was an idiot and then walked out of the kitchen as though it owned the place. I followed her across to the lounge room. The cat circled the room, stopping to sniff here and there. I switched on more lights. At least having this visitor was helping dispel the horror of the evening. It had been bad enough finding the dead man, but there had been people around. Then there'd been that bizarre visit to the pub, and I had been able to push away the shock. But now here I was alone, in a cottage I didn't know, in a town where I was a stranger, and I was frankly freaking out. The cat might be the only thing right now between me and a breakdown.

Having done the circle of the living room, she then walked up the stairs. I followed. Was the cat even house-trained? She walked into the master bedroom and, as she'd done in the living room, she walked around the edges, sniffing here and there as though daring a mouse to appear. And then before I even realized her intention, she jumped up on the bed. She turned around a few times and then lay down and curled into a ball. She didn't sleep though. Those wide, green eyes regarded me, probably the way I was looking at her. Friend or foe?

I didn't know what to do. I ought to put her out so she could find whoever she belonged to, but the fact that she'd been so hungry made me wonder. I'd heard stories about people moving and leaving their pets behind. Had that happened to this one?

Wait a minute. Lucinda had moved. I was positive she wouldn't have left her familiar behind, but there were also stories about pets who traveled miles and miles to return back to the place they called home. Was it possible that this cat who had made herself so at home in this little cottage was Lucinda's?

"Cerridwen?" I asked.

The cat rolled over to its side and extended a paw. I couldn't help it—I laughed aloud. Was she offering the paw to shake? Or just doing a cute cat thing?

It fit though. "Are you Cerridwen? And are you planning to stay here? What about Lucinda? Maybe she needs you."

A familiar wasn't like an ordinary pet. Maybe this one felt that she needed to be here.

I couldn't worry about it now. I'd made one decision, anyway. I wasn't going to put this cat out tonight. I was too happy to have the company.

I got myself ready for bed and crawled in. I had left all the lights burning downstairs, and I had no intention of going and turning them out. If my electricity bill went up, so be it.

I left the bathroom light on too and my door open so that it was not completely dark in here.

I didn't think I'd sleep at all, but Cerridwen, if it was Cerridwen, crawled up the bed once I was settled and curled her body into mine. And the two of us slept.

CHAPTER 8

I woke the next morning with the pleasant feeling of having slept quite well.

In spite of the horrors of the night before, I'd slept right through the night. Apparently, finding a murder didn't trump jet lag. Just as well. In the light of day, the world looked a more cheerful place. Even the ocean wasn't so dark and forbidding a gray but sparkled with sunshine. It was still never going to be a Mediterranean blue. It was more of a bluish pewter today. There were a few clouds in the sky, and seagulls wheeled back and forth. It was a cheerful enough sight. I glanced over at the tower, slightly comforted to know that Lochlan Balfour was in residence. He seemed like the kind of man who could take on a boogie monster, real or imagined.

He must be a very solitary creature, to live there all alone. I wondered if he was one of those high-tech nerds who'd grown up knowing nothing different than their parents' basement and computer games and never learned to socialize. He didn't seem the type, but maybe they didn't have a type anymore.

I showered, did the best I could with my short brown hair, and put on a cheerful outfit: a pink Indian cotton top with embroidery over my most comfortable jeans. I threw on crystals for safety and protection and my chunky necklace of pink quartz to ease my heart chakra. I still felt so sad that Greg was gone.

Cerridwen, if it was she, was still sleeping when I woke, but when I was clearly ready, she got up on the bed and stretched, then hopped off the bed and followed me downstairs.

With no idea how much or when to feed her, I decided to let the cat make her own decisions and put out a fresh can of food. She wasn't as ravenous as the night before and only ate half the tin before drinking some water and then pushing her way through the cat flap in the kitchen door.

I, meanwhile, made a grocery list, including cat food, and breakfasted on yogurt and fruit. I looked at the bread I'd eaten last night but couldn't face it, knowing the man who'd made it was dead.

Outside, Cerridwen was nowhere to be seen. I gave the car a sideways glance and once more hoisted myself onto the bike.

In daylight, it was a very pretty drive down country lanes toward the high street of town. Today there were a lot more people on the street, and most of them seemed to be gathered around the entrance to The Blarney Tome. No surprise, I suppose. I doubted they got a lot of murders around here. At least I hoped not.

I pushed and squeezed my way through the crowd,

getting lots of curious looks. Once again, I felt like the new girl in school. I smiled and murmured good morning and then I was at the front. There was a uniformed cop standing outside the shop, and crime scene tape had been stretched across it. "Good morning," I said.

"Morning, miss," he said. He was young and very firm and looked quite proud of his uniform still. He couldn't have been on the force for very long. I bet this was his first murder.

"This is my shop."

"Is it now. I'm afraid you can't go inside. It's a crime scene."

"Yes, I know. Could I speak to whoever's in charge?"

He seemed to think about this for a moment and then, with a brisk nod, turned from me and opened the door to call in. "The lady who owns the shop is here."

There was some kind of noise from inside, possibly a grunt or an assent, and then in a minute, a guy in a suit who looked like he'd lost too many rounds in the boxing ring came to the door. He showed me his badge. "I'm Detective Inspector Walsh." I could feel the zing of excitement behind me as all the villagers watched me go inside that place that was both horrifying and fascinating at the same time. He motioned me inside, and the young cop shut the door again behind me.

"My name is Quinn Callahan. I've just taken over the shop. Yesterday, in fact. I found, um, I found him."

His gaze sharpened on me. "You're American?"

Well, I could see he'd earned his detective badge. "I am."

"How long have you been here?"

"I arrived yesterday." We both sort of glanced in the direction of the dead guy, or where he'd been. "I know, terrible timing."

"Right. I'd like to take a statement."

I was actually quite pleased to be inside now that the police were investigating. Maybe it was kind of ghoulish, but I'd never seen a crime scene being worked before. Thank goodness.

"We'll go and talk in your office, if that's all right."

I had an office? Who knew? Of course, I pretended I did and told him that would be fine. He motioned to a younger man with very short brown hair who walked toward us.

I let the detective inspector lead the way since I had no idea where the office actually was, and after we wound our way through the overcrowded bookshelves and I resolutely prevented myself from stopping to peruse the titles, I followed his very solid back to the end of the military section and a door that led up a spiral staircase. Before I could say what I was thinking—which was, "Cool!"—I was following him up the stairs. He was slightly bowlegged, and the stairway was narrow enough that his knees nearly hit the walls as we went up. The office upstairs was basically one big room that included storage, an office area, and a seating area with more than a dozen chairs and more stacked at the side of the room. Did someone hold meetings up here?

Piles and piles of books, some brand new in boxes, some clearly used, stood in stacks all around. The roof was peaked, and low windows looked out onto the street front and back. I glanced out one of the windows and found it overlooking the outdoor seating for the pub. It would be handy to be able to check and see how busy the pub was before I wandered over there for lunch. Maybe I could call ahead when I saw my favorite table was free and get them to hold it for me.

The desk had to be at least two hundred years old. It was Regency style, with sets of drawers down either side and a tooled leather top. The wood was beautiful, some kind of fruit wood, I thought, but it, like the rest of the place, was stacked with books and papers. I got the feeling that Lucinda had made a pretty rapid exit out of here. She must've done something as bad as I did to get booted out so quickly. I wondered if I'd ever find out her story and if we'd ever meet.

The detective hesitated and then said, "Do you mind if I sit in your chair? I'd like to take notes."

Oh, of course, he thought my chair was the one behind the desk. I was pleased to see that it looked ergonomic, not some fancy frilly Victorian thing that would give me a backache. At my age, I cared about these things. "No, that's fine."

The other man joined us and was introduced as Sergeant Kelly.

The sergeant moved one of the stacking chairs closer to the desk. There were a few chairs probably meant for downstairs, chintz and overstuffed and comfy-looking but hardly practical to drag around. The hard chair wasn't comfortable, but then neither was I.

I felt a quiver of nerves. I had no idea why. I hadn't killed anybody, but just being interviewed by homicide detectives was enough to make me jumpy. I touched my fingers to my pink quartz and willed myself to breathe in and out.

Sergeant Kelly took notes while the detective inspector asked the questions. He started out by asking my full name and address and, when I gave it to him, looked almost puzzled. "That's the address we have on file for the owner, Lucinda Corrigan."

How I wished I had Kathleen McGinnis here to tell me how to answer these questions. I did the best I could. I stuck to what I knew was the truth without giving him more truth than he could handle. "That's right. Some friends brokered this deal, I suppose you could call it." That made me sound so American. "You see, Lucinda got a job in England, and I was looking for a change." How true those words were, now I came to think of them. "My husband recently died."

"I'm very sorry," he said, more as a rote response than that he could possibly be interested.

"My ex-husband, actually, but we were always friendly."

"You needed a change. Why here? Why now?"

Obviously I couldn't tell him about dragging my husband from the brink of death with a spell I had no business using. Or that it hadn't worked anyway and he'd still died. Or that I was terribly afraid that in flapping those butterfly wings, I'd somehow caused the death of the man downstairs. I stuck with, "Mutual friends knew that I was looking for a change, and so I came here and took over Lucinda's home and her shop. It saved her having to move or pack up. This place will still be here, exactly as she left it, when she decides to return. And meanwhile..."

Meanwhile what? I still owned my house, but when I left the law firm that I so clearly didn't fit into, I'd had no illusions they would ever want me back. Oh, there had been a nice, pleasant lunch where the partners all said flattering things about my efficiency, but while I was a good librarian, I didn't fit into a corporate environment, and we all knew it. I didn't even want to. If Lucinda came back, what would I do? Well,

I'd worry about that another day, when I wasn't being interviewed about a murder.

"I could always go back to Seattle." That at least was true. They hadn't taken away my passport.

"And you were a bookseller in Seattle?"

"No, a librarian." I gave him a tiny smile. "But books are books."

Whether he believed the skills were transferable, I had no idea. His face wasn't given to sharing his emotions. He stared at me out of pale blue eyes, over a crooked nose that had to have been broken about seventy-five times. His face was swarthy. Not enhanced by his crew cut, I might add. He wore his jacket and flannels the way I'd worn my business attire. I had a flash of him in fatigues. Ah. He'd been in the army, and he'd been sent overseas. Somewhere hot. Not my business, and I certainly wasn't about to pry, but he hadn't yet settled into domestic policing.

"Did you know the man downstairs?"

"No. As I said, I only arrived yesterday. I got the bus here from the airport. Went into the grocery store and met Kathleen McGinnis. And then she drove me home to Rose Cottage."

"How did you come to be in the bookshop last night?"

"I had jet lag. I'd had a nap, and I woke up. I was wide awake, and I didn't know what to do with myself. My cottage is only eight minutes away by bicycle. So I rode in and thought I'd just take a look." I went back through my actions as much as I could remember them.

"The front door was unlocked?"

"No. I'm fairly certain it was locked." I went back over my motions. "Yes. It was locked. Because first of all, I put the wrong key in. And the knob didn't turn. I needed to find the correct key in order to open the door. So yes, it must've been locked."

He'd sat patiently while I'd verbally worked that out. What a star witness I was turning out to be. "And describe everything that happened when you walked in the door."

I touched my crystal again and closed my eyes. I saw again the shelves of books and the cash desk at the side and the ridiculous urge I'd had to open it. I didn't tell him that though. "I took a little tour to see what my new place of employment looked like. And when I got to the cash desk, I saw him."

"And you'd never seen him before?

"I'd never seen him before."

"Then what happened?"

I told him that Lochlan Balfour had been walking down the road and he'd come in and then Kathleen McGinnis and that they'd called the doctor. "And then he took care of things and we left."

"Where did you go?"

"Lochlan Balfour was called away by his assistant. He had a business call. Kathleen and I went to the pub." I still thought that was a strange thing to have done after discovering a murder victim. I felt I needed to explain. "Kathleen felt we should have a drink for the shock. And it did give me a chance to meet a few more of the locals."

"And were you shocked?"

What kind of a question was that? "Of course I was shocked. I've never been involved in a murder before."

"How are you so sure it's murder?"

"Are you joking? The guy was facedown in a pool of blood. I don't think he died of natural causes."

"There'll be an autopsy done, of course, but a fall that resulted in a broken nose, internal bleeding, could be natural." It was what Dr. Milsom had said, too. But I'd had all night to think about this. The image of what I'd seen was imprinted on my mind like a photograph.

"The blood was coming from lower than his nose. It was all around his throat and neck area." I waved my hand around the area, demonstrating.

He narrowed his eyes and then nodded. "His throat was slit. But that is not public knowledge, do you understand?"

I did. I had another question. "What was he doing in the shop all by himself? I don't think the dead man had any connection with The Blarney Tome." I looked at the cop. He should know. "Did he?"

He was letting nothing escape him. "We're still making our inquiries, Mrs. Callahan."

"I went back to my birth name after my divorce. And I go by Ms." Chauvinist.

"Well, Ms. Callahan, we'll need to search your house. We can get a warrant if you prefer, or you could voluntarily let us do our search."

"My house? Whatever for?"

He hit me with the steely glare. "Because, like you, I'm curious as to what he was doing in the bookshop. Lucinda Corrigan left, and within days, Declan O'Connor was killed in her shop. Might there be any clues as to why in her house?"

What was he saying? "You think there's a connection between the dead baker and Lucinda?"

"As I said, we're still continuing our inquiries."

Sergeant Kelly had been making notes the entire time, which was kind of unnerving. Then DI Walsh said, "That will be all, for now." He glanced up at me. "Do we have your permission to search Rose Cottage?"

I thought of that pretty cottage and the happy atmosphere I'd felt from the moment I walked inside. Big-footed police officers clomping around poking into everything were not going to add to the happy atmosphere. Good thing I'd brought my smudge sticks. I'd have to smudge the atmosphere after them. Still, waiting for a search warrant seemed like a big waste of everybody's time. So I agreed that they could search.

He didn't look grateful or surprised. He simply nodded. "We'll let you know when we're coming. Obviously, I don't need to tell you, leave everything as it is."

"Can I at least unpack?"

He thought about it. "We'd prefer you didn't. Until we've had a good look at things."

I supposed I didn't really want them pawing through my underwear anyway. "Okay."

I got up and left him there. As I made my way back down, the spiral staircase suddenly seemed less cool.

Was that why Lucinda had left town? Because she was involved with Declan O'Connor?

I nearly tripped down the last few stairs as a horrible thought struck me. Did she have anything to do with his death?

CHAPTER 9

In the bookshop, there were various technicians in jackets, no doubt searching for clues.

When I walked out of the shop, the small crowd parted like the Red Sea before Moses. Or a crowd of healthy people for someone they know to be carrying the plague. I didn't really know what to do with myself, but since I had a crowd watching my every move, I decided to look like I was walking with purpose. I only knew one person in town, and luckily she wasn't standing there gawking. So I made my way to the grocery store as though that had been my intent all along. I did need some groceries. And I definitely needed a bottle of wine.

When I got into Finnegan's, I was relieved to find I was the only customer. No doubt everyone else was hanging around outside The Blarney Tome.

Kathleen was staring down at an open magazine when I walked in but quickly put it aside. She was wearing a yellow cardigan today, and the buttons were tiny daisies. I wondered if she knitted all these sweaters herself. "Quinn. I'm so pleased to see you. Are you all right? Did you sleep?"

"I'm okay," I assured her. "But the police—sorry, the Gardaí interviewed me. It was awful."

"What did you tell them about Lucinda?"

"Don't worry. I stuck to the script. She needed a change, I needed a change, *blah-blah-blah*."

"Good." She searched my face. "Something's bothering you. What is it?"

"I know it's a deep, dark secret why she left. But that man was killed in her bookshop. Is there any connection between her and the victim?"

She appeared genuinely shocked. "What are you suggesting?"

"Nothing. I'm asking the obvious question. And don't think the Gardaí aren't asking the same one."

"Why on earth would you think Lucinda had anything to do with the tragedy in the bookshop?" Kathleen asked.

"Because the death happened in there," I replied. "They wanted to know everything I could tell them about Lucinda, which wasn't much. And now they are going to search the cottage."

Her face screwed up in what I guessed was sympathy. "Oh, you poor thing. Of course, they'll never take their boots off before they come in your house. I suppose it's regulation, but it seems awfully rude."

I wondered how she knew that.

She helped me find everything on my grocery list. When we got to cat food, she did a double take. "You've got a cat with you? How did I not come to see it?"

"It's not mine. It arrived last night and seems very at home in Rose Cottage."

"Goodness. Do you think it could be Lucinda's Cerridwen? That cat always had a mind of its own."

"I think it might be. Would you recognize it?"

She wrinkled her nose. "I might. It's a black cat. They aren't so very different from each other, now, are they?"

And that's when I knew that Kathleen was not a cat person.

I WATCHED HELPLESSLY as two police officers wearing latex gloves went through Rose Cottage as though it were a crime scene. I understood that this was part of their job, but something broke a little bit inside me to watch them going through every drawer, looking at every pot, under the beds, behind the sofa cushions. Not even the books were left untouched. Somebody went through them book by book, shaking them out, looking behind. I think they even moved the bookcases and looked behind those. What did they think was hiding there? The murderer? I felt invaded and uncomfortable.

I'd locked my suitcases. If they wanted to go through my things, they would have to get a search warrant, but apart from confirming that they were mine and moving them so they could look underneath, the police didn't poke into them. For that, at least, I was grateful. Though I didn't see how they could possibly justify going through my things since I didn't even know the poor man who was murdered. But Lucinda had.

Could one of my witch sisters be a murderer? That would

certainly get her sent to England. But we witches weren't big on hiding murderers. Our first rule was to do no harm, and anyone who did harm would not be shielded. At least not by any coven I'd ever been a part of. Besides, in my heart, I didn't believe that Lucinda was a bad person. The atmosphere in her cottage was too content, and I felt her presence almost like a light scent of perfume when someone walks out of the room and you come in right behind them. If I closed my eyes, I could even picture her aura. It was light, the colors of limes and lemons and papayas, citrusy and clean.

Declan O'Connor's body was, as far as I knew, still in the doctor's surgery. Would they send out the body for autopsy or would our local doctor take care of it?

Meanwhile, the Gardaí had combed all through The Blarney Tome, taken photographs, dusted for fingerprints and heaven only knew what else. Most of the books didn't look disturbed. It would have taken them weeks to take every book off every shelf in that overcrowded bookshop. I almost wish they had; I could have used the clean.

It was Tuesday before I was allowed to take possession of the shop. I went in and, after switching the lights on, made sure the sign was turned to closed. I was not yet ready for customers. I brought rubber gloves, a bucket, and every cleaning product Kathleen McGinnis sold. I recited a spell of release, forgiveness, and protection.

If there was a spell for getting blood out of floorboards I didn't know it. Instead, I rolled up my sleeves. I scrubbed, I bleached, I scrubbed some more, and still I couldn't get the dark stain completely out of the floorboards. "A sander," I said aloud. That was what I needed. But who would have one?

While I was pondering, there was a rapping noise on the window. I looked up to see Kathleen, and with her was the man she'd called Danny who had been hanging around Finnegan's Grocery the first day I arrived. She made motions like, "Can we come in?" and I nodded. I stripped off my gloves and went to the door and let them in.

"How's it going?" she asked, looking keenly into my eyes. Today she wore a blue cardigan over black trousers. I felt like a drudge in my old sweats and with my hair bobby-pinned back from my face. Not my finest look.

I had no idea whether the man with her knew we were witches, so I kept my comments superficial. "It's a horrible job," I admitted. "I cannot get the stain out of the floorboards."

She nodded. "I guessed as much. Danny here is the odd-job man around the village. He'll have a look at it and see what he can do for you."

I was so grateful that she had been thinking along the same lines as I had that I led them to the still wet spot behind the desk. You could see the outline of where Declan O'Connor's head had lain on the floor while blood had pooled all around it like a very creepy halo.

Danny shook his head. "Sure and he had a lot of blood in him, didn't he?"

So not helpful.

The man hitched up his trousers and said, "I can bring in the belt sander. I'm not sure how long it will take or how far down the, um, stain goes, but I'll do my best. You may end up with a bit of a dip in your floor, and I'll seal it, but the finish will be different."

"I don't care. So long as you can get every bit of that stain out of the flooring, I'll be a very happy woman. I can always get a rug or something to cover it." What I didn't want was any essence of the dead man right beneath my feet when I was doing business. I was as superstitious as the next witch, and I didn't want somebody else's aura getting in the way of my job. Especially someone who, for reasons yet unknown, had been unpopular enough to be murdered.

He nodded and hitched up his pants one more time. "You let that dry then. And I'll be back tomorrow."

"When do you think I'll be able to open the shop?"

He looked up at the ceiling as though the answer might be printed on it. "Well, that's hard to say. I've got the sanding to do, of course. And then I have to have my tea break, and I always go home for lunch. I have to feed Winifred."

Did he have a sickly wife? An ailing mother? Kathleen glanced at him and then at me. "Winifred's his dog. They're very attached to each other."

"Right."

"So give me a couple of days." He looked back at the spot and then at me. "Call it three days."

Three days to scrub out a patch that was only about two feet wide by a foot? That seemed rather excessive. Since he'd been so keen to mention his tea break, I got the feeling that my new handyman might be a tad on the lazy side. Still, what other choice did I have? I needed the floor done, and I wasn't prepared to sand it myself. So I said, "You have a deal. You'll start first thing tomorrow morning?"

"Well, call it ten."

"I'll be here right at ten to let you in then."

He glanced at me with all too innocent blue eyes, and I gave him my steeliest glance back. I wanted him to understand that I would be watching over him and making sure that he did the job without too many breaks. When they'd left, I pulled down the blinds, not wanting further interruptions and also not wanting an audience to what I had to do now. I pulled out the smudging sticks that I had brought from home. No doubt they had something similar here, but I was used to these. I knew that they were uncontaminated by bad energy and would work. First, I took the bucket of dirty water into the little washroom at the back, where I had a kind of stock room. There was also a little kitchen area with cabinets, a small fridge and a sink. I tipped the bucket of water down the sink and then, taking a lavender-scented cleaner, cleaned the bucket thoroughly and then the sink, and then I poured more water down on top of it. As I did, I said a spell, releasing any essence of Declan O'Connor.

Having done that, I put the bucket and all the cleaning supplies and the rubber gloves outside the back door. I didn't even want them in here contaminating the atmosphere. Then I lit candles. I took a deep breath in and another out. And then I lit a bundle of sage. I let it smoke and smolder a little bit until I could smell the scent, smoky and sweet, and I began to cleanse the space. I began by cupping my hand and letting the smoke drift around me, then moved to the area where Declan's body had lain. And then I walked around, trying to keep from crossing my own steps, tracing a logical pathway so that the energy could follow in a simple line down each row of books and back up the other side and up the spiral staircase, and the smoking sage came with me. I could feel it gathering energy. As I went I said aloud,

North, south, east and west
Cleanse this space and bring peace and rest

Release the negative energy and set it free
So I will, so mote it be

I reached the top area, which was my office and storeroom, and spent time going to each of the four corners, the north, the south, the east and the west, and finally I opened a window and once more invited all the bad energy, all of the previous energy, everything that was stale and stuck and not of mine to go out the window. There was kind of a rush of wind that came behind me and blew out the window. The first time this had happened, I had been absolutely shocked, but I had done smudging ceremonies often enough that I was accustomed to it now. The cleansing breeze was like a psychic broom sweeping negative energy out the door.

I shut the window, and then I walked around and blessed the space, asking for peace, contentment, curious minds and people who loved to read to find what they wanted. I wished myself a safe, stable, and even prosperous stint as the proprietor of this bookshop.

When I was done, I very carefully doused the sage. Having done that, I took the remaining sage outside and buried it in the lumpy dirt behind the shop.

Then, taking special salts blended with herbs for protection, I scattered a line across the doorway both at the back door and the front, and I put a protection spell on the shop. It was all I could do. But I thought it might help. Finally, I blew out my candles, packed everything away and went back to my cottage.

I walked in and immediately knew I had to do another ceremony. Instead of that light citrusy aura that I associated with Lucinda, the place felt heavy, and I sensed the police officers who'd come stomping through with their big boots on and invaded this special, feminine, magical place. They couldn't help it; they had a job to do, but they were gone now, and I needed to get rid of their essence.

However, before I did that, I changed out of all my clothes, went upstairs and had a long, hot shower. Once I was cleansed, I put on a light cotton dress in greens and yellows with a touch of orange. Its colors made me think of Lucinda. Maybe I couldn't bring her back, but at least I could honor her in some way.

I'd deliberately worn the oldest things I'd brought with me to wear while cleaning the shop. I hadn't really brought enough clothes that I could afford to sacrifice any, but I wasn't going to keep those around with all the negative, deadly essence clinging to them like moth eggs, ready to destroy the rest of the place. They would have to be burned.

So I bundled them into a paper bag. I took them outside, and Cerridwen appeared, looking both pleased to see me and hungry. She nosed the bag and recoiled. I suspected she'd stayed out of the way when the Gardaí had been here and waited until I reappeared.

She came inside with me, and I lit a fresh smudging stick. I smudged both of us, and the cat stood patiently while I ran the smoke around her. This was clearly not her first cleansing ceremony. Then, with the burning smudge stick, I walked around every inch of this cottage, especially where I felt the cops had spent the most time. I could feel them almost as though my smudging stick was a Geiger counter and alarms went off when I hit the areas where they'd stood the longest. That was the kitchen and the living room. There was a shed out back, where Lucinda had herbs hanging to dry, but the Guards hadn't spent much time there.

Once I'd gathered up all the bad energy, I opened the front door. I could have used the back door, but that opened into the garden and her herbs, and I did not want any nasty energy dusted across those pretty, fragrant and healing herbs. So I let the negative thoughts and feelings fly past me and out the front door toward the road and then toward the sea, where hopefully they'd be washed away.

That done, I felt much better. I took the smudging stick out to the yard and found a firepit at the back of the garden. I suspected it had been used mainly for burning leaves in the fall. And who knew what else? Making sure no one could see me—and Lucinda had created her firepit in a secluded area, I noted—I called for fire. Flames immediately sprang up. I threw the clothes I'd been wearing into the cleansing flame. And lastly, I threw the smudging stick right on top so that it could burn too. That done, I returned to the house. "Right," I said. "Let's begin again."

The cat looked at me as if to say, *Everything was all right until you got here.*

CHAPTER 10

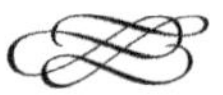

Cerridwen made short work of her dinner, liver this time, while I made myself a simple dinner of salad. After the heaviness of the day, I craved something light.

Once I'd eaten, knowing that my space was cleansed, I began to unpack. Somewhere, in all their digging around through Lucinda's belongings, the Gardaí had unearthed a silk scarf and left it on the bed. It was in the palest blues running into pinks running into purples. It was beautiful and whimsical. And I immediately imagined that Lucinda must be blond. That scarf would look so good on someone with blond hair and blue eyes. I held it to my nose, and sure enough, there was that light, citrusy scent that I had begun to associate with the former occupant of Rose Cottage.

I folded it up and thought I'd tuck it away somewhere in case she returned.

Cerridwen wandered around behind me looking deeply unhappy. She hadn't appreciated those big-booted officers stomping through here either.

While I was unpacking, I thought I'd better make the

space a little more mine. While the dressing table set—the antique comb and brush and mirror sitting on top of a starched cloth—were very pretty, they weren't exactly practical. I decided to put them away and use the space for the cosmetics I used every day. I picked up the mirror and turned it over. It was faded and pocked. "I wish you were a scrying mirror," I said aloud. The nice thing about having a cat was being able to say things aloud and not feel like a crazy person.

And then I looked again. It felt as though the thing was alive in my hand. I turned to look at Cerridwen, who was staring at me with those big, green eyes as though to say, "Now you figure it out?"

"Seriously?" I asked her. "This is a scrying mirror?"

Well done, Lucinda. She'd figured out a way for us to communicate. At least I hoped so. I couldn't wait to try out the mirror, but I would have to wait until night had fallen completely and what moon there was had risen.

While I waited, I'd settle in the front room with the binder of notes that Lucinda had left for me.

Based on Danny the handyman's schedule, I now had three days to make myself familiar with everything I needed to know, but I was a big believer that it was better to get things done sooner rather than later. Besides, I was curious.

Lucinda had left clear instructions about ordering new books, and her hours of operation, the banking and so on, but I had trouble concentrating. I kept looking out the window to check the moon's progress.

I'd always been an impatient witch. The moon, however, was not and took its normal time. While not full, at least it emitted a little light since it was blessedly a clear night.

This would work better during a full moon, but I didn't want to wait. If Lucinda and I were powerful enough, we should be able to manage to communicate. If this was indeed a scrying mirror.

Once the moon was rising, I cast a circle in the living room. I lit candles, and I looped Lucinda's scarf around my neck. I brought Cerridwen in as well for good measure. And then I sat cross-legged. I could hear the sea whispering, and the pale moonlight was coming in through the window. It wasn't enough to overpower the candles, but it was there. I had fire from the candles; I had water and plenty of it from the ocean. I had incense burning for the air, and I was sitting, grounded on the earth. I cleared my mind. I tilted the mirror up so the moonlight touched its murky surface and the candlelight flickered at its edges.

Lucinda, sister dear
Though far away, let this mirror bring you near
Let us open our hearts and our thoughts share
To help each other, this we will dare
As we will, so mote it be

I waited, breathing deeply, my eyes closed, the silk she'd worn soft against my skin. I pictured a woman looking into a mirror and imagined myself looking back. So I remained for close on a minute, and then I felt a presence. I opened my eyes. Her voice was soft as though she were whispering and didn't want to be overheard. "Quinn?"

I couldn't look full on into the mirror without obscuring it with my reflection, so I looked obliquely. I was right. She did have blond hair and blue eyes. "Lucinda, I'm so happy I found you."

"As am I. Have you everything you need?"

"Yes. But I wish we could meet."

Her laugh was as light as splashing water. "We are meeting. Now. But we can't talk too long. They mustn't know that we have a way to reach each other."

By "they" I assumed she meant the powerful witches who controlled us and our fate. "I agree. First, did you leave your familiar behind?"

Cerridwen had begun to purr loudly the minute she heard Lucinda's voice. "Cerridwen? *Is tú mo stóirín.* So she has returned to you. I hoped so. I intended to keep her with me, but as you've no doubt noticed, that cat has a will of her own. She disappeared the minute we arrived here. I'm glad she found her way back all right. I hope you'll be happy together."

"I'll take good care of her. There's something you have to know." As quickly as I could, I told her about the murder.

She sounded genuinely shocked. "I'm so sorry this happened to you on your first day."

"Me too."

I felt that we didn't have much longer. It took a lot of concentration on both our parts to hold this connection between us. "Lucinda, the police searched your cottage today. Is there anything I need to know? Is there any connection between you and Declan O'Connor?"

"No. I'm as surprised as you are that he was found in The Blarney Tome."

My last question was, "Why were you sent away?"

I felt that she wasn't going to answer, and not because the

connection was fading. Finally, she said, "I unwisely provoked a dangerous enemy. I was sent away for my own safety."

There was a dangerous enemy around? Could it be the murderer? "Who was it?"

"I'm not allowed to tell."

I started to say, "But I don't understand." But her voice grew even softer. "There's something else you should know. I couldn't write it down, but there's a special—"

The connection dropped like a bad cell signal.

I concentrated with all my might and finally heard her voice once more, so faintly I could barely hear her, but all she said was, "I must go. We'll speak again. Blessed be."

"Blessed be," I echoed, but now I was talking to a blank mirror.

I STILL HADN'T ADJUSTED to the time change, so I went to bed about eleven and took one of Lucinda's novels upstairs with me. The cover was pink and the author Marian Keyes. Since I was going to be living in Ireland, I should start reading Irish authors. No doubt there were plenty that were heavily literary, but for now I'd had enough of the heavy. I wanted something light and joyous and written for women.

I went upstairs and got myself into bed. Cerridwen had gone out after I'd closed the magic circle. No doubt she had cat things to take care of, but I missed my familiar. It said a lot about my love life that when I got into bed alone, it was my cat I missed.

I gathered my reading glasses and began to read.

Whether it was jet lag or stress or just midlife wakefulness, I didn't know, but I was as wide awake as though it was noon and not nearly midnight when I felt a stinging sensation along the back of my neck.

I put down the book and sat up straight. The protective salts I had scattered across the doorways of this house and all the way around it would alert me if anyone crossed the line without my knowledge. I listened keenly, grabbing my phone and ready to call—who? The Guards were towns away. Who did people call around here when they had a prowler or an intruder?

I was nervous now, and my heart was pounding. I looked for some kind of weapon. There was a heavy brass candlestick on the ornate fireplace mantel in my room. I crept over and picked it up. And then I went to the door and eased it open. I stood there listening.

And heard absolutely nothing. I could sense that I was alone in the house. But that sensation on my neck continued. And then I realized I hadn't only put the protection spell on my house but on the shop, too.

I wasn't the bravest person in the world, but an irrational fury gripped me. I'd spent all day cleaning and cleansing the shop. I was not interested in having my space invaded again. I pulled on my jeans and pulled a sweater over my nightclothes. I pushed my feet into socks and running shoes. I wouldn't go in, I wouldn't be stupid, but I could drive up and see if something was going on in my shop. At the very least, I might be able to take pictures. Perhaps it was Declan O'Connor's murderer come back.

I felt braver now that I had a plan. I didn't want to live in a village where murderers wandered free. Besides, it was such a small town, I bet I could bang on anybody's door and get help if I needed it. Still, I took my phone with me. It was too dark and late to be riding bicycles, so I got into Lucinda's car. It was small and red and faded. This was a car that had sat outside through many days of sunshine and winter and, out here, probably too many days of sea mist and salt water pocking its exterior.

It might be old and faded, but to my relief, the car started the first time I turned the engine. Naturally, it was a standard shift. I could drive a standard—I had learned on one—but that had been years ago, plus I had the whole driving on the wrong side of the road thing to deal with. And shifting gears with my left hand was crazy hard. Still, I felt compelled to see what was going on at The Blarney Tome.

There was no traffic on the road at midnight so I had the whole road to myself. Thanks be. I basically stuck to the middle and drove the short distance back to the high street. As I grew closer, the prickling on the back of my neck increased. Oh, yes. I definitely had an invasion. And I had locked that door behind me. What was the point of keys in this village? Seriously, I was going to get those locks changed. The minute my lazy handyman finished sanding the floor.

Assuming I even stayed in this little village that long. If this murder and mayhem didn't stop soon, I was out of here.

I pulled up in front of the shop. There were a couple of cars parked on the High Street, but everything seemed dark and still. I would have said the entire village was sound asleep if I didn't know differently.

The blinds were down, as I had left them. So it was impossible to tell if there was a light on. I stood at the darkened door and listened intently. I heard nothing. I didn't know if that was good or bad. At least I didn't hear any screams of someone being murdered, nor did I hear any sounds of theft. But what was there to steal? Books? There had been nothing in the till; I'd already checked. And Lucinda had explained that she'd put all the money in the bank just to keep it safe since the whole village knew that her shop was empty. I was to go to the bank, where I had access to the business account, and withdraw enough for the float before I opened the shop for business.

So theft wasn't the motive. What could they be after?

Then I thought, it probably wasn't theft or murder that was going on in here. I bet it was teenagers. They probably had nowhere else to go for their amorous activities and had thought what fun it would be to sneak into the empty shop. I suddenly remembered the joke mug someone had given me at work one birthday. "Librarians do it in the stacks."

I hadn't found the mug amusing, and I certainly wouldn't be giggling if I found some local teenagers doing it in the stacks. I was more annoyed that I'd just finished smudging the place and now they were going to get their sticky romantic entanglement all over. I was going to have to make more smudging sticks, that was clear.

I turned the handle, and sure enough the door was locked, as I had left it. Then I stood there, uncertain what to do. I didn't want to be that girl in the horror movie in the white nightgown who goes down to the basement when there's a serial killer on the loose just because she hears a noise. But neither did I want to be the kind of coward who knew something bad was happening in a shop that she was responsible for and did nothing about it. I looked up and down the street. If I could see a single light in a single house or apartment, I would bang on doors, but there was nothing. If it was just kids making out, the last thing I wanted to do was start my time here by embarrassing them and myself and probably their parents.

Besides, I was a witch. I had powers. I'd be all right. So I took out my key and very quietly and carefully opened the door. It made a loud clicking noise, and as I eased the door open, I froze in the doorway, listening intently.

And I heard voices.

CHAPTER 11

Even though I'd known there were intruders, I was still shocked to hear voices. They weren't moaning, amorous teenage lovers. And certainly not angry voices or even the whispers of thieves in the night. It sounded like some kind of discussion was going on. I was too curious now to leave. I eased myself inside, listened again. Only now did I see faint light coming from upstairs.

In her binder, Lucinda had mentioned that she sometimes offered a story time for children and, if there was interest, a reading group for adults. But it was after midnight, and everybody in town knew the shop was closed. They wouldn't have a reading group. Not now.

And yet that's what it sounded like. I crept to the bottom of the spiral staircase. A woman's voice said, "I think Captain Wentworth should have tried a bit harder. The minute his ship came in and he had his first bonus money, if he loved Anne so much, he'd have gone back to offer for her hand again. And trust me, she'd have taken him."

A second voice, a man with a deep voice, spoke up. "No. It

was his pride, you see. Once a man's been rejected, he's not in a hurry to repeat the experience. And the more he loves a woman, the more tender his feelings are."

This was fascinating. Unless I was mistaken, there were people upstairs discussing *Persuasion,* one of my very favorite novels. Call me crazy, but I didn't think that people discussing Jane Austen were very likely to be murderous. I crept up the stairs. The voices continued. "You men and your pride. She'd rejected another offer which proved she wasn't going to give herself to another man." I had no idea who this woman was, but I agreed with her assessment of Anne Elliot's character. I had reached the top of the stairs. I was certain I hadn't made a sound and I was still out of sight when a man's voice said quite sharply, "Who's there?"

Oh, great. I felt like I was the intruder, and it was my shop. I froze. I didn't know what to do. Run back down the stairs? Walk boldly forward?

"I said, who's there? Show yourself." Now there was an edge of menace to the tone. I swallowed. I couldn't have spoken if I'd wanted to.

Nothing for it. I walked forward with as much confidence as I could muster and came upon an astonishing sight. Lochlan Balfour was standing, staring at me, a leather-bound copy of *Persuasion* in his hands, and a group of people were settled in chairs also holding books. I don't know who was more surprised, my blond neighbor or me. He looked quite stern and very forbidding. I was suddenly reminded of how big he was. The others stared curiously, but I barely noticed them.

"Quinn Callahan? What on earth are you doing here?"

It was so outrageous that I would have laughed if I wasn't

so scared. "What am I doing here? It's my shop. The question is, what are you doing here?"

He had the grace to look a bit embarrassed by that. "We're having our weekly book club. Come and see for yourself."

I felt incredibly nervous, but I somehow knew that if he wanted to tackle me, there wasn't much I could do about it. I'd brazen this out and then get away as quickly as I could. I walked forward. And he must have seen the fear in my face. He said, in a much gentler tone, "You needn't be afraid. We're bibliophiles. Not the most dangerous creatures on earth."

"Unless you disagree violently about a book." It was a weak joke, made with more bravado than humor, but I got a hearty laugh from the assembled readers.

I came closer and checked out an assorted group of people that I had never seen before. Lochlan was the only one who was familiar to me. They looked up politely, but I could see that they were a bit irritated to have been interrupted in the middle of a book discussion. But wait, a couple did look familiar. One was about my age, with short brown hair and a face that was both unremarkable and full of itself.

Another wore evening dress and a colorful paisley silk cravat at his neck. He had a broad, pale face and shoulder-length hair that he wore brushed back. I knew I'd never met him, yet he was familiar.

"I still think Captain Wentworth and Miss Elliot could have been more friendly to each other once they met again, considering they'd been so close," said a woman who was thin and nervous-looking. She wore a fifties-style Chanel suit and held her legs together from knee to ankle as though they'd been welded shut. "They could at least have been friends."

The man with the cravat sighed and turned to her. "Dreary Deirdre, between men and women, there is no friendship possible. There is passion, enmity, worship, love, but no friendship."

"Oh, stop quoting other people's opinions," she snapped.

"Dear lady," he drawled, "To quote our revered Jane, 'a woman especially, if she have the misfortune of knowing anything, should conceal it as well as she can.' Fortunately, you have not that misfortune."

She looked as though she might hit him over the head with her book. And thanks to that exchange, I realized the man looked like Oscar Wilde. Even dressed like him.

"Right, perhaps we'll pause there," Lochlan said.

Each of them held a copy of *Persuasion.* There were five men and three women. They all looked at me politely, but no one said anything. I looked at Lochlan. He was clearly their leader. "I'm confused. Why would you have a book club meeting at midnight?"

I put my hands on my hips as my natural outrage overtook the fear I'd experienced earlier. "And don't even pretend you didn't know the shop was closed, because you were here when I found the dead body. The police haven't allowed me to reopen yet."

I could tell he was scrambling to find a plausible explanation. I hoped he found one soon. Finally, he said, "It's such a habit, you see. We didn't like to break the routine. We started our discussion of *Persuasion* last week, and all of us were anxious to finish this week. We do no harm. We put all the chairs back the way they were when we leave, and any books we purchase, we leave the money for them beside the till."

I was even more confused now. "How long has this club been going?"

They all looked among themselves, and then most of them looked down at the floor or very studiously began to study the pages of a two-hundred-year-old novel as though they'd never seen it before. Lochlan finally said, "Well, it's been a few years now. So, you see, we didn't want to miss an important meeting. We didn't think you'd know anything about it." Then he looked at me strangely. "How did you?"

Ha. "I installed a brand-new security system."

Suck on that.

His eyes glimmered with what I thought was amusement. He knew I was lying. No doubt he was one of those techy guys that could spot a security system a mile away. Maybe he even made and sold them. And if he did, I was totally buying one.

"Would you care to join us?" he asked. Once more I nearly laughed.

"Maybe another time." I held his gaze. Standing my ground.

It was the most ridiculous standoff. The pair of us facing off over a leather-bound classic. Everyone was looking at him as though he'd know what to do next. Finally he said, "All right. We're very sorry to have disturbed you, Quinn. We'll continue our discussion at my place."

"All right."

"Mind you put everything back the way you found it," he reminded them all.

And before my startled gaze, they shifted chairs and put piles of books back where they'd been until he was right—I never would have known they'd been here if I hadn't stumbled on them. They were an odd bunch. They looked as though they didn't get enough sunshine, which was no doubt because they were up too late discussing books. Some looked as though they'd come straight here from a fancy dress party. Or maybe there was a Renaissance fair in the area.

They began to head for the stairs, and I waited until only Lochlan and I were still in the shop. "How did you get in here?" I asked him.

"I have a key."

I held out my hand. "May I have it?"

He put a hand into his pocket and then shook his head as though he was pantomiming *Oh, what a doofus*. "I did have the key, but I gave it to Connie. And she's gone off with it. I'm so sorry. I'll return it to you in the morning."

"I'd appreciate it."

Once they had left, I would make absolutely certain there were no other strangers lurking before I turned out the lights and locked the door behind me. Though honestly, I wondered why I bothered. I might as well have left the door swinging wide open.

CHAPTER 12

When I followed Lochlan downstairs, I found the group standing by the front door, waiting. The guy with the short brown hair was so familiar. I couldn't put my finger on it, but my gaze kept traveling to his face. When he returned my gaze, he didn't seem at all surprised to find me staring. He almost seemed to expect the attention.

I walked up to him. "I feel like I know you." It was the worst line in the world. I hoped he didn't think I was hitting on him.

He seemed gratified at my attention. "Perhaps you've read my work?" He was also American and I was about to ask a few questions when Lochlan grabbed him by the arm and pulled him away and then whispered urgently in his ear. I stood there very confused. What was going on here?

I heard some arguing in low voices, and then the man returned, looking sullen. "I'm sorry. I get that a lot. I've got one of those faces. Everyone thinks I remind them of some-one." He gave a very unconvincing laugh and excused himself. He was wearing a scowl now, and as he went past Lochlan, he said, "Happy?"

I had an uneasy feeling about this bunch. What kind of book club met so late? And snuck in even when the proprietor had changed? Even worse, we'd barely cleaned up after a murder, and here they were discussing a love story. It wasn't exactly delicate behavior. This book club hadn't had something to do with the death of Declan O'Connor, had they?

I stood near the door downstairs to make sure they all left, and I saw the newspaper clipping about the missing author. Of course, the brown-haired man who'd looked so familiar was the spitting image of Bartholomew Branson. Wait, he'd asked if I'd read his work, seemed to expect I'd know him. Could he be the missing author? And if so, what was he doing in a bookshop in Ballydehag? Did he not know there was an international manhunt out for him?

I pulled the article off the wall and walked over to him. "It's you. Isn't it?"

He looked sheepish and then glanced over at Lochlan who shook his head.

"He told you, he's a lookalike. This isn't Bartholomew Branson. This is Dick Musgrove."

I glared at him. "Do you think I fell off a turnip truck? Dick Musgrove is a character out of *Persuasion.* He's the one who goes to sea and dies." I glanced over at Bartholomew. "As you were supposed to have done. But it seems you didn't die at sea. A lot of search and rescue and volunteers have wasted time and resources around the world looking for you. You have devastated fans in mourning. What's going on?"

Bartholomew shook his head. "Believe me, they're not as devastated as I am. I was having the time of my life. On board a luxurious cruise ship that I didn't even have to pay for, giving readings and a couple of lectures. It was great."

"But what happened? When the boat docked in Ireland, you were no longer on it."

He looked as confused as I felt. Lochlan stepped into the breach again. "He's got amnesia. We think he hit his head. That's why he's staying out of sight. He doesn't want the public to know. A famous mystery author with amnesia? It sounds like one of his plots."

I was unconvinced. "Bartholomew has just been telling me about his cruise. He seems to remember that all right."

Ignoring Lochlan, I turned back to Bartholomew. "Can you tell me the plot of one of your novels?"

"Which one? No, a better question, which one is your favorite?" He said it in kind of a flirty way. Oh, I bet he'd had a very nice time aboard that cruise, especially if there were a lot of female fans on board. I tried to remember some of his novels. I knew I'd read a couple. *"Armageddon Force."*

"Good choice. One of my favorites, too. An international thriller where my continuing character, Able Harris, the ex-paratrooper, has to overthrow a drug warlord and rescue his innocent daughter."

I turned it back to Lochlan. "He doesn't seem very struck with amnesia to me. What exactly can't he remember?"

Bartholomew spoke up. "I can't remember my last minutes. I was on deck, at the end of a very nice party where the champagne had been flowing. I went out on deck for a cigar, something I almost never do. I don't smoke, but I'd had so much champagne that a cigar seemed like a good idea. I was looking out at the ocean, and I can't remember anything else."

"Well, that's very specific amnesia, and perhaps the police ought to know about it."

Lochlan looked at me, and his blue gaze looked troubled. "Can I talk to you privately?"

There'd already been one murder in this shop, and now I'd come face-to-face with someone who was missing. Did I really want to be having a one-on-one with a big scary guy, so late?

I did not.

He obviously understood my reluctance. "I give you my word, nothing will happen to you. There are a few things about your shop that you should probably understand. I'm surprised Lucinda didn't tell you."

Since he knew Lucinda, my unease abated slightly. Besides, she'd tried to tell me something that she hadn't wanted to put in the official binder. Could this late-night book group be that thing?

"All right. You've got ten minutes."

He nodded to the others. "You go on. I'll meet you at Devil's Keep." And reminding me of his address really helped calm me down.

He gestured to one of the overstuffed reading chairs. It was so ridiculous, him offering me a chair in my own shop, but I sat in one anyway. I had a strange feeling that I was going to be glad I was sitting down when he explained to me how someone who was missing at sea had turned up in a little bookshop in a small village in Ireland after midnight.

Now that I was looking at him and he had my full attention, Lochlan didn't seem to know how to begin. He put down his copy of *Persuasion.* Clasped his hands around his knee as though he didn't know what to do with them. They were pale, with long fingers. I wondered if he played the piano.

There was a beautiful blood-red ruby ring on one of his fingers. It caught my eye because it was such a gorgeous stone. Then he was speaking. "Lucinda was a very special woman."

Oh boy, was he telling me that they'd been having a relationship? Maybe that's why he was allowed to have book club whenever he wanted.

"We've never met," I said in a cool, clipped tone.

He seemed surprised at that. "Really? I'd assumed you were close. She did give over her home and shop to you."

So none of his business. "You were going to tell me about Bartholomew."

"Right." He let out a breath. "I'm not sure how to begin. I would need, first of all, to have your promise that you will keep whatever I tell you absolutely confidential."

I thought for a moment. I didn't owe this man anything. "If it's something illegal, then I won't keep it quiet. And it wouldn't be fair of you to ask it of me."

He shook his head. "There's nothing illegal going on. A bit unbelievable, perhaps. Some might even say preposterous. But not illegal."

Oh, he really had my attention now. He looked at me quite earnestly. "When I mentioned about Lucinda being special, what I meant was, she has certain gifts." He looked at me with his eyebrows raised. I wasn't going to tell him I was a witch, if that's what he was after. He continued to look at me, and the silence lengthened. "Talents?"

"Maybe she juggles with her toes and sings opera. I have no idea. As I said, Lucinda and I never met."

Again, that cool shaft of humor crossed the surface of his eyes. "You're not going to make this easy for me, are you?"

"I don't really want to make anything easy for you. It seems to me that I have a lot of questions, and you're doing a lot of not answering them."

"Fair enough. All right then. I know that Lucinda is a witch. I'm wondering if you are one too?"

Was this one of the reasons why Lucinda had been run out of town? Had her special status become common knowledge? She'd said she had a powerful enemy. I bet Lochlan Balfour could fit into that category.

I wasn't going to lie, but I wasn't going to jump up and say, "I'm a witch, I'm a witch," either. Some people didn't treat us as well as we deserved. "That's a personal question."

"All right. I don't think I can do anything but tell you something that may shock you."

"I'm not easily shocked."

"How old do you think I am?"

I laughed out loud. "This is your secret? You're going to tell me your age? I don't care how old you are. You're younger than me."

"I doubt that very much."

Okay, I knew I wasn't bad for my age, but I doubt I looked younger than forty on a good day. And I hadn't had many of those recently. I leveled him with a glare. "I'm forty-five years old."

"I was forty-five years old in 1393."

"1393? So you're trying to tell me you were born in..." Okay, math was never my strong suit. "Somewhere around 1350?"

"That's close enough. Yes."

"Well, you are remarkably well preserved. You don't look a day over thirty-eight."

"In fact, I was thirty-five when my life ended in one way and began in another."

I wondered if they'd been doing drugs upstairs. Something that made them all feel like they were different people than they actually were. I couldn't smell anything or see anything. Finally, he said, "Quinn, I'm a vampire."

CHAPTER 13

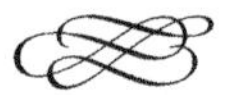

I blinked. I don't think another molecule in my body reacted. It was like I'd been suddenly frozen. All but my eyelids. "A vampire."

"Yes."

"That is the most ridiculous thing I have ever heard. There are no vampires."

"A lot of people don't believe in witches."

"Well, I bet a lot more people believe in witches than in vampires."

What were we going to do, play some stupid game? My entity is more unbelievable than yours? Still, I knew I was right. There were loads of witches, and covens of them all over the world. I'd never, ever met a vampire.

As though he'd been reading my mind, Lochlan said, "We stay very much to the shadows. But you've come across us in life. Probably more often than you realize."

"Why aren't there articles in the paper, then, about mysterious killings and people drained of blood?"

"Because we don't need to do that anymore. One of the

wonders of the modern age is the blood bank. There are all kinds of ways to get blood that don't involve murder."

I felt something strange, almost like a tickle, on my neck. "Well, that's good to know." But was it true? Was any of this true?

"You see, the reason Bartholomew can't remember his last minutes—"

My eyes widened. "No. You're not seriously trying to tell me that the missing writer is..." I couldn't even finish the sentence.

He finished it for me. "A vampire. Yes. One of the members of this very book club, in fact, was on board that cruise. She's a huge fan of Bartholomew's."

I took in a sharp breath. "Did she mur—do that to him?" He'd just said they didn't suck blood out of humans anymore.

"She did, but not in the way you think. Bartholomew's memories are right. He drank far too much champagne, went up on deck to smoke a cigar, and while he was out there, he somehow stumbled and fell overboard."

"On a cruise ship liner? He stumbled and fell overboard? Don't they have like rails and things to stop people doing that?"

"Okay. I've left a bit out. He'd be mortified if anyone knew, but he tried to enact a scene out of one of his own novels."

I wanted to laugh so badly. "Are you kidding me?"

He was trying to suppress his humor too. "No. I'm not. In fact, it was out of that very novel you were just discussing. *Armageddon* something."

I gasped. "Not the famous scene on the battleship? Where the hero has to basically tightrope-walk the rail during a storm? While the evil Russian terrorists are trying to kill him?"

"The very one. He was so drunk that he fell off and down into the water."

"But surely he could've been saved? They have lifeboats."

"Deirdre jumped into the water after him, but he'd hit his head on a lifeboat on the way down. There was barely any life left in him. He wouldn't have survived. She made a split-second decision. Let him die, or give him this eternal half-life that we enjoy."

"You are telling me that one of his fans turned Bartholomew Branson into a vampire." I wanted to make absolutely sure I was hearing him right.

"Yes."

"Deirdre? Wasn't she the one in the Chanel suit?"

"She was."

I was curious though. This was such a small village. "Who else knows your secret?"

"No one. Lucinda was a trusted friend. I'm hoping you will become one, too."

After Lochlan left, I stayed behind and wondered. Could he possibly have been telling the truth? I had no idea, and according to him, there was no one in the town I could ask. Did Kathleen know or had she guessed?

I wandered up and down the aisles. I was in a bookstore, after all. If there was any place I was going to get information about vampires, it was here. Sure enough, as I wandered through the stacks looking at the various books, I came across an entire section of vampire lore. It was a pretty sizable selection, considering the size of the bookstore in this town. Was that for the glamorous resident in the castle?

I hovered over the titles. Picked up Bram Stoker's *Dracula,* obviously, and somehow I didn't think I'd ever read it. There were also titles about the truth and lore behind the vampire legend.

I didn't know what the protocol was for me borrowing titles out of the bookstore, but I assumed, as the person running it, I should at least be allowed to read the books in here without having to buy them. I'd read these titles and bring them back. At least then I'd know what was between the covers.

I headed back to my cottage and, making certain to lock the doors behind me, went straight through to the front room and looked out the window. There was the castle, as large and brooding as ever. I wasn't very surprised to see lights go on in one of the lower floors. Seemed they'd continued their book club after all.

There was a lot about my new neighbor that I didn't know. And probably didn't care to know.

I had believed I was coming to a sleepy town in the middle of nowhere, and what I had discovered was a murder right in my bookshop and then a nest of vampires who ran a late-night book club. I'd only been here a few days. I couldn't imagine what horrors were still to be discovered, if I even made it to the end of a week.

I went to bed, but couldn't sleep. I pulled out the stack of books and began to read. I thought I'd put Bram Stoker's *Dracula* aside for another day and concentrate on a book that was more about the history and lore of the vampire. What I discovered was there was no standard vampire. Some claimed a stake to the heart would kill them. Some sources said no. Every culture had some kind of myth that involved drinking blood. Had Vlad the Impaler really been a vampire? Sources couldn't agree.

About four in the morning, I glanced out the window and saw lights were still on at the castle. One thing was certain, and all the sources agreed on it, vampires were nocturnal. According to my spying out the window, that had turned out to be true.

Cerridwen returned from wherever she'd been and settled beside me on the bed. I finally fell asleep, but not surprisingly, I didn't have a restful night. My dreams were dark and frightening, and I woke the next morning wondering how my life had ended up such a mess.

FEELING there could be no more surprises in store, I rode my bicycle into town and parked it behind my shop.

Danny the handyman was as good as his word. He showed up at ten, or thereabouts, for the next three days. He loved to chat, and unfortunately, he couldn't sand and talk at the same time, so I quickly learned to find things to do upstairs when he was around. Which wasn't a lot. If he wasn't off on a tea break, he was waiting for a coat of this or that to dry. Still, he was easy company and I had lots to do, learning the bookshop, figuring out how to use the cash register, and trying to make sense of the extra stock upstairs.

Danny knew everything about everybody in town, though, and as long as I kept him supplied with cups of tea, he kept me supplied with intel on the locals. I learned that Giles Murray had been a fashion photographer. He'd met Beatrice when she was modeling, and the pair of them decided to turn their backs on the fashion industry and move here. They chronicled local weddings, took school photographs and, according to Danny, had a store on the internet where they sold calendars and greeting cards. "And things of beauty they are, Quinn. I've lived here my whole life and never thought how beautiful it is."

I agreed. "Sometimes you need to see things through someone else's eye to really appreciate them. What about Lochlan Balfour?" I asked my garrulous handyman.

He put down the pot of wood coating he was painting over his newly sanded spot. "Mr. Balfour is from a different world," he said, waving the paintbrush about as though he could paint that world.

"Really?" Was Lochlan's secret not as safe as he believed?

"Oh, bless me, yes. He's that rich that when the local school was going to have to close because there wasn't enough money to keep it open and not enough students so they were going to bus them to the next town, he gave the money himself, he did."

"That was generous. But he's probably got so much of it, he barely noticed."

"Well, that's as may be, but the community noticed. I've always felt myself that nobody notices his money as much as a rich man does. Stands to reason, really. It's probably how he got rich in the first place."

"And what of his ... associates?" I couldn't think of a better word.

"Oh, them as works for him, you mean? I hear tell he gives them housing as well as a generous wage. Well, Devil's Keep is big enough, and what would one man do living there all alone?"

He didn't seem to think it was at all peculiar to have all those odd, pale-looking people living in the castle. I thought Lochlan Balfour had spent his money wisely. The villagers were so busy being grateful to him for the school and whatever else he paid for that they turned a blind eye to the castle.

Most of Danny's chatter was harmless gossip about people I didn't know. Besides, there were too many Bridgets and Marys and Seans for me to keep straight. I'd figure it out as I got to know them all.

I was curious about his thoughts on Declan O'Connor, though, and asked him what he knew of the dead man.

Once more, he put down the brush. I noticed he splotched it on an old section of floor, not that I supposed it mattered. "Declan O'Connor was a very good baker." He glanced at me under his bushy white eyebrows as though wondering what else he could safely say to me.

"I'm not easily shocked, you know," I assured him.

"Well, I don't like to speak ill of the dead, but there was some trouble a while back." He glanced around as though to assure himself that we were, in fact, alone in the empty shop. "Woman trouble."

"Who was the woman?"

"Bridget Murphy was her name."

"Is that the woman who teaches Irish dance?"

"No, that's Bridget Donovan."

"Right. It's the one whose daughter moved to London and married the pastry chef."

"Ho, no. That's Bridget O'Keefe."

"Oh, I give up."

"Bridget Murphy hasn't lived in these parts for going on five years. Ye're not likely to meet her."

I resisted the urge to scream. "And Declan O'Connor was friendly with Bridget Murphy?"

"That was the rumor when her man and Declan had a fistfight, and then they moved to Galway."

"But, more recently, was he involved with anyone?"

"He was off to see his sister an awful lot, ye see. People did start to wonder if it was really his sister he was after visiting."

"Have you told the police? I mean, the Gardaí?"

"Someone will have, I'm sure."

The police had been a notable presence Sunday and Monday, but today I hadn't seen a hint of them. I felt a keen interest in this case since the man had been found in my shop, and I wanted to see justice done.

I also wanted to settle in Ballydehag without wondering if there was a murderer on the loose.

CHAPTER 14

I opened The Blarney Tome on Tuesday, ten days after I'd arrived in Ballydehag. It was a bright spring day, and I picked tulips from the garden and brought them in to work, putting them in a jug I'd found under the sink in the tiny utility room. I flipped the sign to open and, just to make it absolutely clear that I was ready for business, I fixed up a shelf of titles and put it out on the sidewalk.

I had no idea if Lucinda had done that before, but there was a small bookcase that looked perfect for the purpose. I included fiction, nonfiction and some children's books. I even included a couple of titles by Bartholomew Branson. I also put out a free box where I put paperbacks that were out of date or a bit dog-eared.

It was a beautiful day, and my little bookstore quickly began to get attention. Other retailers popped in to wish me well and introduced themselves, often bringing me small gifts. A young woman with a riot of curly hair and a nose stud came in with a coffee and a scone in a paper bag. "I'm Tara," she said. "My partner and I run Cork Coffee Company.

Sounds like a chain, but we've just got the one at the moment. Anyway, I thought you might like a latte and a scone. Welcome to Ballydehag."

I was touched by her thoughtfulness. I thanked her, and she said she had to run but she'd be back to browse when she had more time.

I sipped the latte and found it excellent. People walking by stopped to glance at the titles or rummage through the free box, and a few came in to browse. A woman with small children bought several children's books, and an older couple bought a military history for him and a literary novel for her.

Rosie Higgins, who with her husband owned the butcher's, popped in to wish me well. I asked her how Eileen O'Connor was doing. I hadn't seen the widow since the death. She shook her head. "Such a terrible thing. Liam's running the bakery. She can't face it yet." She leaned in to say more when another woman walked in holding a pretty glass vase filled with spring flowers. "Why, Karen, aren't those lovely."

The woman she called Karen had red hair tied back from her face. She wore trendy glasses over her brown eyes and wore a yellow blouse, a flowered skirt and lots of costume jewelry. "Oh, I see you've already got flowers," she said, looking at my tulips.

"Oh, but those are so much nicer." And they were. She had a much more artistic eye than I and had made a proper arrangement out of tulips, daffodils and bluebells with some greenery. "And the vase is so pretty."

"I'm Karen Tate. I run Granny's Drawers."

I smiled at the name. "I've seen it. You're down the block on the other side."

"That's right. Welcome." She looked at Rosie. "We'll have to organize a girls' night to introduce Quinn properly."

"Excellent idea. We'll do that. Now I must get back, or himself will be wondering what's happened to me." And with that, Rosie left.

I moved my tulips to a small table between two armchairs and gave this new arrangement pride of place on the scarred wooden cash desk.

"I can't stay long, either, just wanted to welcome you and wish you well." Karen hesitated and then added, "I hope it hasn't put you off, finding Declan like that."

"It wasn't the greatest first impression," I admitted.

"We'll definitely have that ladies' night and take your mind off it. I take it you're single?"

"Yes."

She nodded. "Me, too. We'll have to stick together then. Maybe go to the pictures one night or out for a meal."

"I'd like that." I would too. I was going to have to make some friends in this town, and discovering another singleton about my age was a great start.

About midmorning, I was shocked to see Lochlan Balfour walk in. In the middle of the night, I hadn't really believed he was a vampire, but seeing him walk into my shop at eleven o'clock in the morning, I noticed how pale he was and how, somehow, out of place he seemed in the daylight. He didn't seem to flinch from the sunshine though.

He came in and said, "Good morning. I see you decided to open today."

"I did. I don't think I can stay home forever just because there was a murder in my shop."

He walked toward me and went behind the desk. He

looked down at where I'd thrown the area rug over the spot where the poor man had lain dead. "You've disguised the spot well."

"I'm surprised to see you in daylight."

"Don't believe everything you read."

I walked him to the entrance, and as he walked out, he glanced down at the case of books and turned back to me, amused. "Are you trying to flatter our newest member of the vampire book club?"

"Well, Bartholomew did seem a bit sad not to be a living celebrity anymore. I thought he'd enjoy it."

"I'll make sure he sees it."

CHAPTER 15

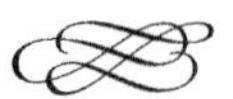

Thursday, the weather turned, and Cerridwen was waiting at the car when I decided to drive to work.

I had decided to work on the children's section today and was already thinking about ways to encourage reading. When I opened the door, there was a piece of ordinary letter-size white paper that had been folded and pushed through the mail slot.

I picked it up, thinking this was the sort of town where there'd be a street fair or a family barbecue and everyone would be invited in this rather charming and old-fashioned way. I was already half-smiling, wondering what this invitation would be and feeling pleased to be included. I took it to the cash desk. I flipped on the lights and straightened it out and looked at it properly. It was a printout of a photograph. A woman was talking with a man, both of them standing in front of a car. It looked as though they were about to kiss.

I had no idea what the picture was for, and I didn't recognize anyone in it.

There were printed words beneath. "Not just friends." That's all it said.

I looked closer, and I realized I did know one of the people in that picture. That was Rosie Higgins. But the man she was about to kiss didn't look like Mr. Higgins.

I didn't know what to do. Was this some kind of a joke? Somebody playing a peculiar prank on the new girl in town? If so, I didn't even get it, and it certainly wasn't funny.

I was contemplating what I should do when Kathleen McGinnis walked in. I looked up and sighed in relief. "Oh, am I glad to see you."

"I'd take that as a compliment if you didn't sound so desperate. Whatever's happened, girl? You look as pale as your shirt."

I didn't answer her. I just pushed the piece of paper toward her. "You probably shouldn't touch it. There might be forensic evidence on it." I'd been pushing the thing all over the counter. But how was I supposed to know?

She glanced at me and then down at the page. She wore the same green sweater she'd worn the first day, but the buttons were different. Plastic shamrocks now buttoned her up from throat to belly so only the collar of a pale green blouse was visible . She read the note. And then peered closer. "What a vile thing to send."

"Is that what I think it is? I'm assuming that man is Declan O'Connor. I never saw him in life, but it looks like the guy who was facedown in my shop."

She nodded. "Oh, yes, that's Declan all right. And the woman with him is Rosie Higgins."

"The butcher's wife."

"That's right."

Well, I didn't know any of these people very well, but "Not just friends" was a pretty obvious message. "Is someone suggesting they were having an affair?"

She put her head from side to side as though trying to judge whether it might be true or not. "He did have a reputation with the ladies."

I looked closer at the photograph. Declan O'Connor would never be confused with a good-looking man. He was overweight, balding and his ears stuck out. "That guy?"

A smile floated across her face. "Don't be fooled by appearances. Especially not post-mortem appearances. He was a charmer, that one."

"And what did the butcher think about that?"

"I doubt he knew. I never heard a whisper of it. I'd have said Rosie wasn't the type, but perhaps there is no type."

"So whoever pushed this under my door is what? Trying to cause trouble in that marriage?"

"Or more."

I stared at her. "Are you suggesting that the butcher might have found out about his wife and the baker? And done something about it?" Butchers and bakers. "Soon we'll be suspecting the candlestick maker," I couldn't help but add.

"It's not a joking matter, Quinn."

She was right. But why send this to me? "What do I do with this?"

I was so new in town. I didn't want to be the one that blabbed about infidelity in a village I was planning to call home.

She shook her head. "You've got no choice. You'll have to give it to the Gardaí."

"But why me?" I whined in an "it's not fair" voice. "Why push it through my door?"

She looked at me as though thinking that was a fair question. "Well, this is where he was found."

"And that wasn't bad enough? Now I'm the mail depository for cheating spouses?"

"Not all cheating spouses, dear. Just that one. Maybe whoever sent this liked the symmetry of putting the message where the victim had been."

"But if this picture is suggesting that the butcher killed the baker, then who took the picture?"

"I don't know. Someone who saw something and doesn't want it known that they're the ones who are tattling on Sean, I suppose. Sean Higgins isn't a man you want to get on the wrong side of."

Great. Just shove that task on me then.

She seemed to think about it. "Also, you're the one person in town who had no reason to kill him. You'd barely arrived when it happened."

Lucky me.

"You best call the Guards."

Not a sentence you want to hear first thing in the morning. Still, she was right. I pulled out my phone and opened the drawer to find the card of DI Walsh. I made the call, and he said he'd be right down. Of course, right down meant it would be at least an hour till he arrived. Not knowing what to do with the paper, I found a large plastic bag, and using the tail of my shirt so that I wouldn't get any more fingerprints on the evidence, I managed to slip the paper into the bag and tuck it into the drawer beneath the cash register.

Then I put a bright smile on my face and happily helped

my customers for the rest of the morning. I knew that this rush of business wouldn't last. Most everybody who came in was clearly there to check out the new woman in town and maybe get a gander at where the baker had been killed. Still, I was either a great saleswoman or they felt guilty, because nearly everyone bought a book. Sometimes it was just a tatty secondhand, but I had brand-new hardcovers to sell too. I felt that my first week in business was going to be quite a respectable one, profit-wise. At least I hoped so.

Andrew Milsom, the doctor, came in. I greeted him and weirdly caught both of us glancing at the spot where Declan had died, as though remembering the place where we first met. "How are you holding up?" he asked me.

"I'm all right," I said. This was the automatic response I'd been giving everyone.

His eyes looked like they'd seen everything. He held my gaze. "Really? I was an emergency room physician. A shock like that, you don't easily get over. If you need something for anxiety or to help you sleep, come by my surgery."

I doubted very much he was trying to drum up new business, as he was the only doctor in town. I thought he was being genuinely kind. "Thank you." He didn't know I had my own ways of relaxing and dealing with sleeplessness. I did not have to turn to drugs when I had spells and tisanes and a few potions of my own.

He searched my face and seemed satisfied that I wasn't on the brink of emotional collapse. "I came to see about that fishing book Lucinda ordered for me."

"We do special orders?" I asked. It was a stupid question. It was a bookstore. Of course we ordered special books in. I didn't remember seeing that in the binder she'd left, but then, as I knew from the vampire book club, she hadn't told me everything.

"Well, Lucinda did. She usually kept her special orders in that cupboard behind you."

I'd opened all the cupboards, but I supposed that one hadn't registered. I'd seen books. Big deal.

Sure enough, when I checked, there was a fat book still wrapped in cellophane called *Fishing in Ireland.*

"Could that be it?" I asked him all innocently. It was not only the only book sitting in the special order section, but it had his name on it.

"I think that must be it," he replied quite jovially. This man clearly loved his fishing. He paid by credit card, and before he left, he reminded me that his door was always open if I wanted to talk about what had happened.

I thanked him once again, and he left.

A couple of minutes later, the door opened and in came the two detectives. Fortunately, there was no one else in the shop. I pulled out the incriminating evidence and pushed the plastic bag across the cash desk. DI Walsh nodded, looking quite pleased that I'd managed to put it in plastic. Though they were probably happy just to have a lead. "Did you handle it at all?"

"I'm afraid I did. I came in and it was on the floor, folded. I thought it was an invitation or an announcement of some kind."

They put on gloves and took the paper out of the bag. "That's the victim. Do you know who the woman is?"

"Yes." I hated doing this. "It's Rosie Higgins. She and her husband run the butcher shop across the street."

The two looked at each other. Sergeant Kelly asked, "Shall we go pay a visit to the butcher?"

The older detective tapped his blunt fingers on the wooden cash desk. "No. Ms. Callahan, would you be good enough to call over at the butcher's? If the wife's there, see if you can find a reason to get her over here."

I nearly squeaked in alarm. "Over here?"

What was I, crime central? This was a bookstore, not the police precinct.

DI Walsh didn't look any happier with the idea than I was. "I don't want to talk to her in front of the husband. And they work together and live together. If you could get her over here, I can talk to her quietly upstairs."

No "please," no "do you mind." I supposed he was requisitioning my shop the way they used to do in the war. If that was even legal anymore. Still, I understood his dilemma, and I didn't want to embarrass the poor woman any more than he did. So I agreed.

"You'll have to watch the shop, then, until I get back."

CHAPTER 16

They both looked alarmed, but I didn't care. I walked out and crossed the street, then walked down the block to the butcher. The sun had come out, and I tried to enjoy the warmth and brightness of the day, even as I dreaded my errand. Ballydehag Meat and Deli was painted white with black lettering. A sign in the window promised, "Famous Fresh Sausage Made in House." I walked in, and there was Rosie Higgins at the front counter, packaging up some sausages for an older couple. They were chatting away about the weather, and it was such a charming Irish village scene that I would have happily stood for ages listening if it wasn't for this awful feeling in my chest. Behind her, an open doorway displayed Sean the butcher at work in a blood-stained apron. He wielded a big cleaver in his hand as he hacked up some poor dead animal. I shuddered. I did not think I would be buying sausages today.

When the couple left, Rosie looked at me with an expectant smile. "Good morning, Quinn. And what can I do for you on this lovely morning?"

My voice was low and quick and nervous. "That book you ordered? It just came in. You should come over to my shop and pick it up."

She looked puzzled, as well she might, since we both knew she didn't have a book on order. I held her gaze, and then I glanced very significantly at where her husband was happily chopping dead things. And then I brought my gaze back to hers. I whispered, "The police are in my shop and want to talk to you."

She glanced behind her, but her husband butchered on, oblivious. She nodded sharply. "I'll be right over."

Message delivered, I headed back and told the police she was on her way.

I had no idea what she said to Sean, but within five minutes, she came into the bookstore with her shoulders hunched around her as though ready to ward off bad news. Or a blow.

She glanced around. "Where are they, then?"

"Upstairs. They want to ask you a few questions."

She closed her eyes and hunched even deeper into herself and then, with a brisk nod, made her way to the stairway at the back of the shop. It seemed that everybody in town knew the layout of my store. I heard her footsteps going up the spiral staircase. She sounded as though she were climbing a scaffold.

I tried not to listen, but I have quite acute hearing. I didn't hear many individual words, more the rise and fall of voices. The male asking questions and the female answering in a fluttering tone.

After about twenty minutes, she came down again. Alone. There was no one in the shop. I thought for a second she was going to walk straight out as quickly as she could, but she seemed to change her mind and came over toward me. "Quinn, please don't tell anyone."

"Of course not. I didn't mean to cause you any trouble. The note was pushed under my door. I didn't know what to do."

She almost seemed like she hadn't even heard my words. Like she waited for my lips to stop moving and then spoke again. "I never meant to hurt my husband. But Declan was such a charmer. Always one for a laugh. And, I don't know, he made me feel young again. Beautiful."

She blushed and looked like she'd dropped twenty years. "Sexy."

I thought Declan O'Connor must be a womanizer indeed if he thought this rather plain middle-aged woman was sexy. But it wasn't my business, and I tried very hard not to judge. We all did things we regretted, and no one knew that better than I.

Naturally, I was filled with nosy questions. Had her husband found out? Could he have killed his rival in a fit of jealousy? But I didn't have a law enforcement badge or any right to ask.

However, Rosie wanted to unburden herself, and I guessed that me being both a woman and a stranger here made me easy to talk to. The butcher's wife was nearly in tears as she leaned close. "They asked me so many questions. Quinn, I believe they think I might have killed him."

Yes, I thought so too. And it didn't seem like a bad theory either. Perhaps she could read my thoughts in my face. She shook her head, looking tearful. "Why would I kill him? All he ever did was make me feel good. Like a desirable woman.

It's been years since my husband looked at me like that." She thought a bit longer. "Decades." She smiled sadly. "Treated me like a queen. It was grand. He had a special wine he'd bring along when we got together. He was planning to leave Eileen and we'd go off together, as soon as Liam was on his feet. We were in love, you see."

I wasn't a police officer, and it wasn't my place to grill her, but the man being found dead in my shop gave me a certain interest in this case being solved. Besides, I was now a resident of this village. If there was a killer on the loose, I'd be a lot happier if they weren't on the loose. Apprehended would be good.

"Do you know who might have done it?"

She blinked away her tears. And then looked at me sharply. "That's what the police asked me, too. Are you working with them?" I don't think she'd given that view of the problem a thought. "Oh. I see what you mean." She glanced at the section of Irish travel books that I had behind the till as though the answer might be found there. "I wouldn't have said anyone would want to hurt him."

It was a delicate subject, but I had to ask. "If he was spending time with you, is it possible he was also spending time with someone else?"

"Oh, no. He was devoted to me."

"What about Eileen?" If the man was planning to leave, could his wife have tried to stop him from going, permanently?

But Rosie shook her head. "Eileen never knew a thing about it. We were that careful. Well, she's a friend of mine. I wouldn't want to hurt her."

Right.

"And your husband?"

"All he notices is his dinner and the telly. I could dance naked in the lounge, and he'd tell me to move so he could see the football match."

Before she left, I had another question. "I'm trying to find out who has keys to the shop. Do you?"

She blinked at the sudden change of subject. "Yes. I think so. And I believe you've got ours. It's handy, isn't it?" Two old ladies had stopped and were poking through the free box right outside. "I'd best get back."

I promised again that I wouldn't tell a soul, and she left the shop. As I watched her hunched figure hurrying back toward the butcher, I thought, a guy with big strong arms like that and more knives and cleavers than probably anyone else in Ireland could certainly have killed the baker.

The ladies came in and thanked me for the free books and said how glad they were that the bookstore was remaining. I thought they'd support it better by actually buying a book but naturally didn't say so. After they left, there was a flurry of business and then a lull. I got a thrill every time I rang up a purchase. I wondered if that feeling ever got old and hoped not. I wanted to make a go of this, both for Lucinda's sake and mine.

The detectives were still upstairs. The interview had finished some time earlier, and I hadn't seen them come down. I thought I'd better go upstairs and see what was going on. I experienced a moment of dread as I put my foot on the first of the spiral stairs. If that woman was a murderer, was it possible I'd find two more dead bodies above me?

I shook my head at my own foolishness. I would have heard something if there'd been violence going on upstairs.

I'd been aware of tension in the air, but nothing like death had occurred above me. Not in the last hour. Still, when I got to the top of the stairs and saw the two of them talking quietly, a notebook open between them, I was thankful to see they were alive. They both looked up when I arrived, and you wouldn't have known it was my shop. They acted like I was intruding on them. I said, "I was just going to make a cup of tea. Would you like one?"

The icy atmosphere immediately thawed. "That would be very nice, thank you," DI Walsh said. The other detective just nodded.

Right, two cups of tea then.

There was a tiny kitchen beside an even tinier bathroom in the very back of my shop, near the back entrance. I'd found it stocked with tea, both Irish breakfast tea and three varieties of interesting-looking herbal teas that were clearly homemade. Presumably by Lucinda. There was a packet of biscuits that didn't look too old. I made the tea and put out the fresh milk that I had bought and kept in the tiny fridge and some sugar cubes I also found in the cupboard. Having made the tea for the two of them, I decided I really needed a cup too. I took it all up to them on a tray. They thanked me, and as I was about to leave, DI Walsh said, "Ms. Callahan. Stay a moment."

Oh crap. Now what?

"It's a bit unorthodox, and I hate to ask it of you, but could you go across and ask the butcher to come over here?"

I felt all the horror of being dragged into something that was absolutely none of my business and extremely embarrassing. "Are you kidding me? But then he'll know his wife has been having an affair."

He didn't look too pleased to have me questioning him like that. He gave me a cold stare and said, "Will you do it? We can't make you, but we thought it would be easier if the villagers saw you going into the butcher rather than the Gardaí."

Okay, they were actually trying to be gentle. So I nodded. "Do you want me to go now?"

"If it's convenient."

I couldn't think of anything less convenient than hauling a bear out of his cave. Especially one who worked with sharp knives for a living. What if he was the murderer?

CHAPTER 17

For goodness' sake, Quinn. It was broad daylight, I was on the high street, and all the shopkeepers and the people who lived here seemed to have nothing to do but spy on each other. Kathleen had warned me they were a bunch of curtain-twitchers.

I hoped Sean Higgins wasn't the butcher-the-messenger type.

I went back downstairs. Took five minutes to drink my tea, which I really needed now. And then I headed out. I did feel watched as I crossed the street. Again.

Once more, I entered the butcher shop. Rosie looked up and when she saw me went as pale and clammy as one of the skinless chicken breasts quivering in the case. Our gazes connected. I gave a helpless shrug. "Is your husband available? He's needed at the shop."

She swallowed. Closed her eyes. And I saw her hands grip each other hard. Then she nodded. She turned and shouted into the back. "Sean? Quinn would like you to go across to the bookshop."

Her husband was enormous. In his short sleeves, the tattoos on his arms looked like warning flags. He came out and said, "What do I want with the bookshop? The only thing I ever read is the news."

"Please," she said in a shaking voice.

He looked at her and then at me and then said, "I'll just wash the blood off me hands."

A line I really could have done without.

He was back out in a minute, with his bloodstained apron off, thank goodness, and a jacket on. His hands looked clean enough. He followed me outside. "What's all this about then?" Not suspicious, just wondering.

I didn't know what to say. "I think you'll understand when you get there."

He paused in the middle of the road. I'd gone two steps before I realized he wasn't following me. I turned around and stared back at him. He had a very uncomfortable look on his face. "Declan O'Connor was found murdered in your shop. What are you? Some crazy man-hater? Are you going to call all of us blokes into your shop and murder us one by one?"

Well, they do say that the best defense is a good offense. I couldn't stand here in the middle of the road arguing with this man that I wasn't a murderer. So I went closer to him. To my amazement, this enormous, muscular butcher looked a bit nervous. I had a feeling that if he didn't know how many people were peeking out their windows and watching us right now, he'd have taken a step backward.

I lowered my voice. "The police want to talk to you. They're in my shop right now. They asked me to come and get you so that everybody in town wouldn't know that you were being interviewed."

He looked slightly relieved. Then concerned again. "Me? Why would they want to talk to me?"

"I don't know. I sell books. They've taken over my upstairs as their temporary office. That's all I know."

He nodded once and then strode forward. Once we got inside my shop, I showed him where the spiral staircase was. He was probably the only person in town who didn't know the complete layout of my store. I heard his heavy tread going up the stairs and then, once more, the murmur of voices. I was so going to have to smudge that space again when they were done. First murder, and then the investigation? This atmosphere was going to be rank with bad feeling.

CHAPTER 18

When Cerridwen and I arrived to open The Blarney Tome the next morning, I willed the day to be one of book sales, meeting more residents of Ballydehag and of me becoming more comfortable in my new role.

I'd talked to Greg's teenage daughters last night and, besides being grateful to social media that I could see their faces and talk to them, so it felt almost like a real visit, I saw that they were grieving honestly and healthily for their dad while also getting on with their lives. I heard about boyfriends, lack of boyfriends, school, and only a bit about Greg. This was good. They were moving on, which made it easier for me to do the same.

I saw my departed ex-husband in the way Ashley, fifteen, put her hand to her chin while thinking. She had his analytical mind. Hannah, at thirteen, had his round, hazel eyes and his sarcastic humor. They were the closest I had to daughters, and I loved them. I showed them Cerridwen and my cottage, and both vowed to come and visit.

So I was in an upbeat mood when I unlocked the shop

door. However, my mood plummeted when I saw the folded paper on the floor.

"Really?" I cried aloud, glancing up and down the deserted high street. "Really?"

No one answered my cry of frustration. This time, I didn't touch the paper. I used the tweezers from my makeup kit to pick it up off the floor. The page opened as I did, and I saw a photograph very similar to the first one. It had probably been taken on a phone or a digital camera, printed out on the most ordinary paper with just a date and time and another snarky comment.

The woman in the picture was Karen Tate. The man coming out of what I guessed was her home was Declan O'Connor. Apart from the date and time was one line: "Look who's been getting into Granny's Drawers."

I hadn't been inside Karen's shop yet, I'd only walked by, but it appeared to sell a combination of antiques and second-hand finds and probably a load of junk. It was the kind of shop I would have loved to go in and browse some afternoon when I had a few hours and nothing to do. In the front window was a display of costume jewelry, a jug and basin, some old furniture, and some vintage dresses. I couldn't imagine what I'd find inside when I started to rummage around.

Someone had obviously been spying on Declan O'Connor and the owner of the shop. Just like they'd been spying on Declan O'Connor and the butcher's wife. Maybe they had pictures of everybody in town doing things they probably shouldn't be doing. It was a bit unnerving.

Once more I called DI Walsh. Once more he and his side-kick, Sergeant Kelly, made the drive into town.

And once more, I was dispatched to Granny's Drawers to suggest that the proprietor might like to come to my bookshop. There were three people in the store when I walked in, so I pretended to browse. Two of them looked like retirees with not a lot to do. They were two women, probably in their seventies, and they were rooting through a box of mismatched china, each piece priced at one euro. I got the feeling that they probably spent a lot of time rummaging for bargains when they had nothing better to do. Another woman was flipping through a rack of secondhand clothes. She had a focused look on her face. I knew that look. I bet she had somewhere she needed to go and she was trying to find just the right blouse or new dress or accessory to freshen up her wardrobe without spending a lot of money. Karen Tate looked up when I entered and said, "Good morning, Quinn. Can I help you with anything special?"

Not wanting to alarm her or start gossip flying, I said, "No, thanks. I've been dying to come in here. I just thought I'd take a break and have a quick browse."

She walked up to me, which I felt was special treatment. "It's great to see you here. How are you settling in? I've been meaning to organize a girls night, but I don't know where the time goes."

The woman who had been browsing through the clothes looked up and gave me a nod and then went back to her browsing. The two older ladies said good morning and then went back to the one-euro box of wonders.

"I'm doing my books for the accountant." She made a face. "Have a browse and let me know if you need help."

Fortunately, Karen had a shelf of old books right at the back near where she was working at a small desk. I followed her and pretended to study the titles. "I'm always drawn to books," I said. "Occupational hazard." It was probably the lamest thing I could have come up with, but I couldn't think of anything else. At least if I stood near the books, I could speak to her in a low voice and no one would overhear me.

She gave me a curious look from behind her laptop. "I'm not competition, you know. People just bring books in sometimes as part of their clearing out."

"Oh, sure. I just love books."

I spent a minute or two looking through old, dusty volumes. She didn't have any paperbacks, I noted, only hardbacks. They ranged from cookbooks to a couple of decorating titles that had to be at least twenty years old.

I picked up one of the cookbooks and flipped through the recipes. I lowered my voice and said that the two detectives would like to talk to her. And that they were in my shop.

She went pale. "What?"

"I'm sure it's nothing," I said. "I think they're talking to a lot of people. They sent me because they didn't want to shock you." She still looked worried, but I could see her trying to compose herself.

She glanced around at the patrons in her shop and then said, "I can't leave now. I'll be along in a few minutes. I'll have to wait till my customers leave and then lock the shop."

"Of course." I left, and very shortly afterward, the two older women came out.

Before I'd even crossed the street, they caught up to me. They'd clearly abandoned their one-euro finds. "Quinn Callahan, I'm so pleased to finally meet you. I'm Edna O'Grady. I'll be along to your shop very soon. I've been meaning to get over and introduce myself. However, my husband hasn't been too well. We only live in the next block. So it's very easy for me to come to the village to do my shopping."

The other woman now piped up. "And I'm Clara McPherson. We're so pleased that you were able to come to our little village. We don't know what we would have done without a bookshop."

Even though I'd never seen either of them yet in the shop, I liked that they appreciated having a bookstore. In a town this size, I thought they were very lucky to have one. I said, "You must come and have a look around. Tell me if there are some titles you'd particularly like me to bring in and I'll do it. Also, if you wanted to start a book discussion club or something, I think we could accommodate that."

I already had one going late at night. Why not have one in the daytime?

"Oh, that's such a good idea. Lucinda tried one a few years ago, but I don't think it ever took off. Still, we've a few more people in our village now. More of us are retired with not enough to do. A book discussion group could be grand. I think your timing could be very good, Quinn."

Then Edna glanced behind her, making sure, I supposed, that no one was in hearing distance. "It would be nice if you'd be a bit friendly with Karen, the owner of Granny's Drawers. She's been very down in the mouth since the murder."

They looked at each other and nodded, filled with excitement, perhaps, at a local murder. I didn't suppose there'd been many murders around here. Ballydehag was like a postcard for the perfect, sleepy Irish village. Pretty and serene.

I couldn't help thinking about that paper that had been

pushed under my door. As innocently as I could, I said, "Were they great friends then? She and the murdered man."

They looked at each other again, and I could tell they were dying to gossip. I could almost see the words bubbling up until they couldn't be held back any longer. It was Edna O'Grady who spoke. "Well, I'm not one who likes to speak ill of the departed," she said in a way that suggested to me quite the opposite. "But I did notice Declan O'Connor seemed to spend rather a lot of time at Granny's Drawers."

"Oh, Edna, you mustn't talk so. You know very well he was only fixing a fuse or some such thing. Something had gone and, as she's a single woman, Declan O'Connor looked out for her. That's all."

"Not that I'm saying there was anything untoward. But he did seem to come and go at very odd hours."

"Honestly, Edna. There was nothing to it."

"You can say that if you like, but I've eyes in my head, and I know what I saw."

I didn't really want to take part in this gossip session that seemed to be turning into a quarrel and, naturally, didn't have anything to contribute since I wasn't about to tell them about these strange notes that were being pushed under my door. Then I thought, nosy old women who didn't have enough to do? Might Edna O'Grady be sending those notes?

Did these old gals even have cell phones?

I decided to try an experiment. "I've forgotten my mobile. Can you tell me what time it is?"

Crafty, I thought, until they both showed off their wristwatches and gave me the time down to the second. I had to remember that not everyone had come of age when the mobile phone pretty much took over from the wristwatch.

"But is that time accurate? I always find my mobile phone does so much better a job."

They both shrugged and obviously thought I was peculiar, no doubt being American. Each of them pulled out a very modern-looking cell phone. They each checked the time against their wristwatch and nodded, looking satisfied. "Yes, we gave you the correct time."

"Great," I said with bright friendliness. "I'd better get back to my shop then. Look forward to seeing you again." And with a wave, I headed back to the bookstore. Could someone retired and bored have taken the photos? They were very clear about showing Declan and his women in clearly compromising situations. I suspected whoever took them had taken their time to get exactly the right shot. Retired busybodies would have all the time in the world.

I didn't have long to wait until Karen Tate came in. She looked furtive and guilty. I didn't blame her. I felt furtive and guilty too, and I hadn't done anything. I told her to go on upstairs, where the detectives were waiting.

While I was worrying about what was going on upstairs, Lochlan Balfour walked in.

His penetrating blue eyes studied my face. "Something's troubling you. What is it?"

His tone was gentle, and I felt that he genuinely wanted to know. Speaking with Hannah and Ashley, and briefly with Greg's widow, Emily, had reminded me how far from home I was. I had no one to talk to here. Maybe that's why I answered honestly. "I feel so confused. I thought I was coming here to run a bookshop, and now there's been a murder." I glanced up at the ceiling. "The police are up there, interviewing one of my neighbors."

"It's a trying time for you." He glanced down exactly where the body had lain. "But you are here to start a new life and run a shop. The Guards will catch whoever did it, and we'll go back to normal."

I knew something that the police didn't, and it was what had been worrying me. "Could one of you have killed Declan O'Connor?"

His amusement was gone, and a flat, cold expression replaced it. Man, looking into those blue eyes was like looking into a glacier. "By my kind, I assume you mean the undead?"

Even him using that term made me shiver. I nodded mutely.

He looked a bit disappointed in me. Suddenly I wished I hadn't said the words. But I had, and it was a reasonable question. He looked again at where that body had been. And I couldn't help it—my glance followed his. Lochlan said in a low voice, "First of all, if one of my kind had killed that man, you wouldn't have found him in a pool of blood. He'd have been drained dry. But nowadays, we don't need to hunt in order to stay alive. There are many places we can meet our nutritional needs. In fact, we have a special relationship with some doctors who provide us everything we could require."

"Really?"

"Also, donated blood is only kept for about forty days, then it's disposed of."

"I didn't know that."

"Instead of letting it be destroyed, we buy the blood. The money helps fund the Irish healthcare system."

I really didn't want to know the details. But while I trusted Lochlan was telling me the truth, he had a new vamp in town who might not know the rules. "What about Bartholomew Branson?" I was blundering into completely unchartered territory here, and I didn't know exactly even what I was trying to say. "He's a brand-new vampire. Might he be overwhelmed with the need to feed?" I'd seen vampire movies and TV series that all suggested the newest vampires could be the most dangerous.

Lochlan Balfour rolled his eyes. "Training Bartholomew to hunt would be like training a mouse to vanquish a lion. It's a good thing he was turned so recently. In the old days, he never would have made it."

I'd never thought about that. I always assumed all vampires were terrible blood-sucking monsters. "You mean?"

He nodded curtly. "Back in the old days, anyone who was squeamish or unable to hunt didn't last very long."

"Oh."

"Let me explain something to you. How can I put this? Imagine a steak dinner, served in a fine restaurant."

"Okay." I got hungry just thinking about it.

"Now, imagine you could go to a fine restaurant and order that steak, exactly to your liking, and eat in pleasant surroundings when you felt hungry, or you could hunt the animal, slaughter and butcher it before you could eat. Which would you choose?"

Well, that was a no-brainer. I saw what he was getting at. "You're suggesting that getting blood from a blood bank is easier than hunting?"

"Vastly. We can even order the blood type we prefer. I'm an A positive man, myself."

"I'm type O." Just so we were clear. I'd never been so pleased to be ordinary.

His lips twitched. "Duly noted. So, have I convinced you that neither I nor any of our book club did away with the town's baker?"

"Yes. I'm sorry. I just didn't know."

"I'm glad you asked. Now we've cleared the air, there's something I want to ask you."

CHAPTER 19

Okay, I admit I felt a little flutter of attraction. He might look a lot younger than I was, but we both knew he was actually hundreds of years older. What did that do to the older woman/younger man vibe, when a guy looked young but was actually ancient? Maybe I should be more worried about the vampire/witch divide than the visible age difference.

Anyway, I hadn't come here for romance. Quite the opposite. If he asked me out, I was going to say no.

He was gorgeous, though, so I felt a pang of regret when he said, "I've come to issue an invitation to you."

I'd never been any good at turning men down, even when I'd been younger and it had happened more frequently. "Oh, I'm not really—"

He interrupted me, looking a little embarrassed. I suspected that if he could blush, he might have done. "The group talked it over. We'd like to invite you to join our book club."

"Oh. The book club. Really?" On the plus side, he hadn't

asked me on a date, but as invitations went, this one wasn't exactly making me jump up and down with joy. "Don't tell me—you're planning to have this meeting in my shop?"

Now I understood why he looked slightly embarrassed. He nodded. Once more, that disquieting look of amusement crossed his cold, blue eyes. "Lucinda used to come. We always enjoyed her perspective."

Now he was buttering me up. "And if I hadn't stumbled on your last meeting, would you have bothered to invite me?"

He seemed to think about it. "Probably not."

"Didn't think so."

"But now we know you're a friend, like Lucinda was, we would like you to come."

"And I suppose if I said no, and furthermore, you're not welcome to meet in my shop, what would you do then?"

"I hope you won't forbid us your shop. This is where we've been meeting for years. We like it here. We don't do any harm. And, you know, all of us are enthusiastic book buyers."

I didn't really have a philosophical reason why they couldn't use my shop. But I did think it was a bit cheeky to invite me to take part just so they could use it. I was about to tell him he could just go ahead and use the shop and not worry about it, but then I stopped. How often does a person have a chance to sit with a bunch of vampires and talk about novels? In my brief time here in Ballydehag, I hadn't felt overwhelmed by a love of culture. In fact, there was no other book club that I knew of in town. I admit I was sorely tempted. "I tell you what, I'll come for tonight's session and then we'll see."

"Wonderful. And we thought, as a mark of respect and welcome, we'd let you pick the next book."

"Really?"

"Yes. We'll be finishing *Persuasion* tonight, and then we'll choose our new title. So take your time and think about what you think our group might enjoy."

I WAS EXCITED. I even tidied up the shop. I thought about baking, but then I realized who my readers were. Anything I'd baked they wouldn't want to eat. And what they probably wanted to eat I didn't want to provide. Instead, I cleaned. I found a vacuum in an upstairs cupboard and gave the upstairs a good going over. I tidied the desk and made sure the blinds were down.

While I had the vacuum out, I decided to run it over the downstairs too. It was amazing how much dust and dirt tracked in from the street. I was so virtuous, I even got out the attachment for corners and edges. As I was running it along the edge behind the cash desk, it sucked up something that got caught and fell out again with a rattle. A small pebble? I leaned down to pick it up and found it was a mother-of-pearl button.

For a long time, I stood looking at it winking at me from the palm of my hand while the vacuum motor droned on.

THE VAMPIRE BOOK club settled in a circle and pulled out their copies of Jane Austen's *Persuasion.* Lochlan said, "We didn't quite get to finish our discussion last week, so let's finish up with *Persuasion* tonight, and then we've invited Quinn to pick the next book for our discussion group."

"Welcome, Quinn," said the woman I remembered was Dierdre, the one who'd turned Bartholomew Branson into a vampire.

"We've a couple of members you didn't meet." Lochlan gestured to a woman with bright golden curls that hung past her shoulders in what I suspected was a wig. Her pale cheeks were rouged, and she wore a long dress that dipped low to show an ample bosom. "Mary Boyle."

Before I could say hello, the Oscar Wilde look-alike said, "Really, Lochlan. Have some respect. If a lady cannot be beautiful, she likes to be titled. My dear, you are in the presence of that great literary hostess, the Countess of Cork. Lady Cork to you."

I looked at Lochlan. What was I supposed to do? Curtsy? I settled on, "It's nice to meet you."

"And of course, you know me. My genius precedes me."

"I know that you look and sound like Oscar Wilde."

He threw back his head and laughed. "Oh, but you're wonderful. Why should I be myself when I can pose as someone less interesting?"

There was a young woman with purple hair and a nose ring called Zoe and half a dozen more vampires. I couldn't keep track and hoped I'd get to know them as time went on.

They all looked at me and nodded, approving. I had the strangest feeling that they'd been told to be on their best behavior with me. No doubt they felt, as I did, that this was a trial. Maybe Lucinda had welcomed a group of vampires to discuss literature upstairs, but I wasn't entirely sure that I was going to continue that tradition. I mean, vampires!

There was some shuffling and discussion of the Jane Austen classic, but the discussion was stilted. Everyone was entirely in agreement with everyone else's comments, which weren't exactly original. I didn't say much except to defend Anne from a complaint of peevishness, but I suspect Oscar had only said it to rile us up. After about twenty minutes, the whole discussion petered out, and then everyone looked at Lochlan.

"All right," he said. "Good discussion. Now, we need to pick a book for next week. Quinn?"

"Well," I said, looking around and gazing at each of them in turn. They didn't look particularly dangerous. They looked quite eager to hear what I had to say. "I've given it a lot of thought. And I think what I'd like to start with is Bram Stoker's *Dracula.*" He was Irish, after all, and I thought I'd enjoy reading the horror classic a lot more in the company of vampires.

There was a stunned silence. And then, after about a full second, they spontaneously erupted into laughter. I cannot even describe to you how strange it was to see a dozen vampires doubled up in laughter. They looked like a bunch of six-year-olds when someone had told a bathroom joke.

Lochlan held it together better than most of them, but I could see his suppressed mirth in his twinkling eyes and the way he held his mouth rigidly closed.

"What!" I said when the laughter died down a bit.

"Well, obviously you don't know us very well, but the book's utter nonsense," Lochlan said. "Someone fed Bram Stoker the most ridiculous lies, and he believed them."

Yet again more laughter.

"Okay," I interrupted. "I get the idea. He didn't do his research very well."

"More than that, he gave vampires a much worse name than we deserved." There was a bit of general muttering, and then a grumpy man who hadn't said much uttered, "But we took care of him."

They weren't laughing anymore. There was a kind of a smug, secret smile that they all shared. I didn't know how a bunch of vampires would have taken care of a writer they didn't approve of. And I really didn't want to know.

"Okay, then." I thought rapidly. "You don't want to read a book about vampires. You obviously like the classics, but what else would be a good choice? I don't want to be choosing a book if I don't even know what you guys have read."

Bartholomew put up his hand, as eager as that annoying, smart kid that always sits at the front of a class. "I recommend we discuss one of my books. I mean, how lucky are you to have the actual author sitting amongst you. I can tell you all about my research and where I get my ideas and—"

He stopped talking when a copy of *Persuasion* hit him just behind his left ear. "Ow."

"For the last time," Lochlan said, "we're not going to discuss one of your books. We've been alive for hundreds of years. We don't want to read about greedy corporations, secret armies and crooked politicians. We like escapist fiction."

Bartholomew slumped back in his chair and subsided into a pout.

No wonder they were trying to get me to choose their books.

"Maybe we should read something American," Lochlan said, glancing at me. "In honor of Quinn here."

I looked around at them. What book would appeal to this group of vampires from different eras? They didn't seem to appreciate newer fiction. I don't know where the idea came from, but I said, "What about *The Scarlet Letter?* By Nathaniel Hawthorne."

As one, they all turned to look at Lochlan. Could these vampires not even pick a book without his approval? He must be one powerful dude.

He nodded. Slowly. "What made you choose that one? I don't think we've ever read and discussed it."

There was a general shaking of heads. "I've never even heard of it," said Zoe of the purple hair. I didn't know when she had been turned into a vampire, but presumably whatever her past, it hadn't included studying the classics of American literature.

Lochlan ignored her and looked at me curiously. "What made you choose a novel about forbidden love?" His eyes glittered a little, and I wondered if he was getting ideas. I wanted to shut that down right away. Not that he wasn't gorgeous, but I couldn't handle so many crazy changes already in my life. A romance with someone who was undead seemed just one step past crazy.

Why had I come up with that one? "I honestly don't know. The idea just popped into my head."

"Well, it's a good one."

Everybody agreed except Bartholomew Branson, who muttered something about literary snobs. However, no one paid him any mind.

I did feel sorry for him though. It must be so hard to go

from public fame and massive book signings and being a pop culture celebrity to being forced to stay inside and never be seen. He was worse off than most of the other vampires because he was so recognizable worldwide. The downside of fame.

"I've got a copy of this at home. Who else has one?"

They all looked around and then shook their heads. "Okay, if you've a copy downstairs, Quinn, perhaps Zoe could have it." Then he turned to me. "Lucinda used to order in whatever extra copies we needed."

"Okay. I'll order the books in the morning."

"Good. Let me know when they're in, and I'll pick them all up at once. Twelve copies should do."

Lucinda had left me instructions on ordering books, but I didn't know if vampires got a bulk discount. Strangely, she hadn't left me a single hint about her very peculiar book club. How was I supposed to know the rules?

One thing was certain. With a famous literary hostess, two authors and a group of fascinating characters from every era, book discussions were going to be interesting.

CHAPTER 20

It was late when I returned to the cottage, but instead of getting ready for bed, I brewed a calming tea. I lit a fire for cheer more than warmth and settled with my tea. I took the mother-of-pearl button I'd found when cleaning and placed it on the table.

That would teach me to clean so thoroughly. Now I had a dilemma.

That mother-of-pearl button, or one very like it, had been on Kathleen's sweater the day I first met her. The day I found Declan O'Connor murdered in my shop.

When she'd come back during that awful hour when I'd found the body, she was wearing a coat and dress. No sweater. And later I'd seen what I was certain was the same green cardigan, but she'd changed the buttons.

Of course, there could be a hundred innocent explanations.

But, unfortunately, there was also one very disturbing explanation for how this button had turned up near the murdered man. Kathleen had been there before me that night.

Had Kathleen been sleeping with the baker? Why hadn't she said anything to me? I wouldn't say we were friends—we hadn't known each other long enough—but we were sisters. Why would Kathleen not have told me what was going on? I could think of only one reason, and it chilled my blood. What if Kathleen didn't want to tell me of her relationship with the murdered man because she was the one who'd caused his unfortunate demise?

Cerridwen came in from her nighttime roaming and curled up on the rug in front of the fire. "How can I find out if Kathleen's been lying to me?" I asked the cat.

Her answer was a contented purr.

I felt pardonably irritable. I'd been sent to the other side of the globe for trying to save a man from death—what kind of punishment would Kathleen deserve, if she'd caused a death? The first rule of all witches was to do no harm. Slitting someone's throat was what I would call big harm.

I didn't know what to do. I had decided, when I left Seattle, that I was going to back off from my craft. Deep down, now that my ex-husband was dead, I could see that my sisters had been right. Trying to save him, when his destiny was set, had been foolish. I might have been driven by genuine compassion for him and his daughters, but love had blinded me to the obvious. I had been rash and interfered where I had no business. Had that butterfly flapped its wings all the way over to Ballydehag, Ireland?

Had me saving my ex-husband somehow caused Kathleen to kill a man? If my theory was true, that practically made me an accessory to murder.

I sat there for a long time unable even to summon the energy to go upstairs. I was awash with guilt.

I didn't know what to do. Did I tackle Kathleen and tell her what I knew? Or did I pretend I knew nothing and, acting devious, try and discover the truth for myself? I had no idea.

I wished I'd left the vacuum cleaner in the cupboard.

I DRAGGED into work the next morning bleary-eyed and with no decisions about what to do with that button.

To my surprise, I'd barely opened the door when Lochlan walked in. He looked as fresh and well turned out as though he'd slept eight hours when I knew how little sleep he got by on. According to my mirror this morning, sleeplessness and worry were written on my face in new wrinkles.

"Good morning," I said, feigning cheerfulness. "What brings you here so early?"

"I've something to return." He looked sheepish and presented me with a silver pen that I'd been using upstairs on the desk. It wasn't mine. Lucinda had left it. He also returned a pair of amethyst earrings that were mine. I'd taken them off when I'd been on the phone upstairs and slipped them into the top drawer of the desk.

I looked at the items on my desk and then up at Lochlan with a question in my eyes.

"It's Mary Boyle. Lady Cork. She can't help it, you see. She's a kleptomaniac."

Since I'd moved to Ballydehag, I was beginning to think nothing would ever surprise me again. "Oscar Wilde told me she was a famous society hostess in her day."

He nodded. "And that she was. Glittering soirees. Everyone went to her parties. She was witty, engaging, encouraged writers and was a friend of Dr. Johnson, though they did argue." He smiled, and I realized he must have been at these parties. "But if she was invited to other people's homes, she tended to pinch the silver."

I couldn't stop the laugh. "What?"

He grinned at me. "It's true. Her servants would return things they didn't recognize, but once word got around, she didn't get many invitations."

"I don't even have words."

"Maybe lock your desk before the next book club meeting."

I'd been too tired to put on earrings this morning, so I slipped the amethysts into my lobes. "Thanks. I guess. Is that guy really Oscar Wilde?"

"To be honest, I'm not certain. He could be an excellent poser. Or he could be the genuine article. Whichever he is, he's very entertaining."

He was studying my face, no doubt noticing how bad I looked. "What's troubling you, Quinn? Was it too much for you last night?"

"No. It's not that. I enjoyed the book club. It's like nothing I've ever experienced before. Obviously."

"Something's upset you. What is it?"

What was really bothering me was the thought that Kathleen might know something about this murder. That she hadn't told me she was having an affair with Declan O'Connor. She was the only friend I had in town. I didn't want her to be guilty of murder. But even as I felt the urge to unburden myself to Lochlan, I realized I couldn't do it.

Kathleen was a sister, a fellow witch. I had to talk to her first.

So I told a big, fat, white lie. "I'm having trouble with the ordering process. I haven't been able to order your books yet."

"Lucinda didn't leave you any instructions?" He shook his head. I thought he was a little sad. "Lucinda left very suddenly and left no forwarding address. I would have liked to say goodbye to her and tell her how much she'd meant to all of us, running the bookshop and welcoming us. But she didn't give us that chance."

"I know. I didn't get a chance to say goodbye to anyone in my life either. Once you screw up, in my world, they take care of you pretty quickly."

"So it seems. What did you do wrong, Quinn?"

"Do you really want to know?" Once again, I realized I didn't have anyone to talk to here. I was tired, worried. My defenses were down. In truth, I felt sorry for myself big-time.

So I told him about Greg getting sick. How unprepared he'd been for death, how his daughters had begged me to save him and, finally, how I'd done what I knew was wrong. Lochlan was a very good listener. He wasn't twitchy. He didn't seem like he was waiting for my lips to stop moving so he could jump in and talk. I felt that he had all the time in the world to listen, and so I felt the great relief of being able to unburden myself. When I'd finished, he said, "I'm sorry."

Of all the things I'd heard, just that simple "I'm sorry" was one of the most sincere. I nodded, feeling lighter somehow.

"I've lost a number of loved ones over the centuries. Each one breaks your heart in a new place."

"Do the wounds ever heal?"

"Yes. And the scars fade, but they never go. My only

advice is not to fight grief. Learn to live with it and try to hold on to the happy memories."

I did have happy memories of Greg. Lots of them. And he'd left behind Ashley and Hannah.

"I was thinking about that book you chose. You're a witch. You've obviously got enormous powers and a kind of special knowledge that not everyone shares. That made me wonder why you would choose *The Scarlet Letter.* Why that particular novel."

He was right. I hadn't really thought about it. I'd grasped for an American classic after they'd mocked Bram Stoker. "It just sprang to mind."

"More than, say, Edgar Allan Poe, Louisa May Alcott, Toni Morrison or Mark Twain? Any of a hundred other American authors."

I felt he was leading me somewhere, and then I understood what he was getting at. "You think it's a clue, don't you? That my subconscious came up with that novel as a way of finding out who killed Declan O'Connor."

"I think it's possible."

"But why do you care? You've made it very clear that neither you nor any of your kind had anything to do with his death. Why not leave the Gardaí to solve it?"

It was a moment before he answered. I saw Giles Murray walk by with Beatrice, as usual, on his arm. No doubt they were headed for the coffee shop. "Quinn. When you look ahead at your future, what do you imagine?"

I had no idea what this had to do with my question. "I don't know. I just got here. My future is trying to figure out if I can fit in in this little town and make a life here."

"Beyond that. Looking ahead to all the years of your existence."

Now I had an inkling of what he was getting at. "I've probably got another forty years left if I'm lucky. I think about trying to do good work and building a life for myself. Retiring one day and growing herbs. Making candles and potions. Deepening my craft."

He nodded. "Forty years is"—and he snapped his fingers so they made a loud crack in the quiet—"the snap of your fingers or the blink of an eye to us. So we get bored. And helping solve a murder is a good project. I've been puzzling over it. Why would anyone kill Declan O'Connor? He was a good baker. He was a friendly chap in the pub. Who would want him dead and why?"

"That's why you think I chose *The Scarlet Letter.* You think he was involved in a forbidden love affair and the other party felt so wracked with guilt that it was as though they were being burned by it. And so they lashed out."

"I think it's a theory worth pursuing."

He knew this village a lot better than I did. "What about his wife?"

"Eileen O'Connor is devoted to their son, Liam. Did she know her husband was carrying on? I don't know. They always seemed content together."

"She seems genuinely distraught now that he's gone."

I was sure that what I was doing was slightly unorthodox, and the police would have a fit if they knew, but somebody had pushed those notes under my door, and I was fairly certain that Lochlan Balfour wasn't going to be gossiping around the village. I said, "I've been getting notes."

While I couldn't show him the originals, I'd snapped photos on my phone which I pulled up.

He studied them. "As long as I live, and it's likely to be a very long time yet, I am endlessly surprised by human behavior."

CHAPTER 21

Later that day, Eileen O'Connor came in. She looked smaller than I remembered her. The big personality and laughter were gone. She glanced around as though wondering why she'd come in.

"Eileen," I said, walking forward. Gently, I asked, "How are you?"

"I'm doing all right, thank you. I'm on my way to the church. I help with the flowers, you see. But when I passed your shop, I thought I'd try and find a novel to read. I'm not used to having all this time on my hands. I'm usually at the bakery at dawn, but now, I sit at home all day. I can't watch any more telly. I thought I'd try a novel. I want something cheerful."

I knew how she felt. After Greg died, I'd been so grateful to stories that offered a few hours of escape. "Do you want to browse, or would you like suggestions?"

"I'll just have a wander." And she headed down the biography aisle.

Seeing her here made me realize how important it was to

get justice for her family. I had possible evidence, but a button on its own wasn't enough. While I was convinced the button belonged to Kathleen, I needed to understand what she'd done.

Finally, I decided to invite her to my cottage for tea. I'd be serving my specially created truth tea. I felt a little nervous issuing the invitation, but Kathleen sounded pleased to be asked, so then, of course, I felt guilty. It wasn't that I was trying to trick my sister witch, but I needed to know the truth.

So I headed home straight after work. While Cerridwen watched me, looking slightly perturbed at my actions, I prepared my special tea. I got my ingredients together, and cleansed the space and prepared my circle, making sure to close the circle behind me to keep the purity in and the bad stuff out. I then lit a white candle. I sat before it and watched the flame. It was important to focus, to think of that flame burning away all the extraneous thoughts in my head and helping me to find clarity. Normally I would do a spell over the tea when it was finished, but I didn't want Kathleen to hear me, so I asked for guidance in seeing through the mists of lies and finding the true light of truth.

That done, I found the most traditional china in the cottage and opened a packet of chocolate biscuits. I put on some nice, light music, something I'd found in the collection that Lucinda had left behind her. It was some sort of collection of Celtic ballads sung by a woman with a truly beautiful voice. I found it soothing.

When Kathleen arrived, she was already talking as she came in the door. "What a day I've had. Run off my feet. Why does everyone buy their groceries on the same day? Oh, and Danny was driving me mad. I swear that man has no home to go to. He spends half his time hanging about in my shop. If it wasn't that I won't have his dog in the grocery, he'd move in there, I swear."

"It must be nice to have somebody to talk to when there aren't too many customers."

"Well, that's true and it isn't. Sometimes a body just likes her own company."

She was wearing one of her endless sweaters. This one was a cherry color over a pretty, flowered dress. No one would ever call Kathleen McGinnis a beautiful woman. I doubted if she'd ever attained pretty in her day, but she was easy to talk to and good company. And she did have very pretty, green eyes.

I said, "I've got the kettle already boiling. Let me finish making the tea."

She asked if she could help me, and I told her to sit down and relax. Back in the kitchen, I poured the boiling water over my prepared mixture and, casting a quick glance to make sure she hadn't followed me, I very quickly whispered the spell again. I really needed this to work.

I took the tea out with both honey and sugar and the plate of cookies. I set it down and poured her a cup. As I passed it to her, I said, "This is my own blend. I'd very much like your opinion of it. It can be a little bitter, though, so I highly recommend adding some honey."

Her eyebrows rose at that, and she looked at me a little more sharply than I would have liked.

She didn't bother to taste it, simply took some of the honey and stirred it in. She sniffed it before she drank and looked at me again with a curious expression on her face. "Marjoram, a little mint, I think—is there a touch of lavender? And a deep note I don't recognize." She was good, I'd give her that. She took a tentative sip like a sommelier tasting a mysterious bottle of wine that's lost its label. "Oh, you're right, Quinn. It's got a dark streak of bitterness in it." Then she glanced up at me. "That's not centaury, is it?"

Before I could either pretend that I hadn't put the bitter root into her tea, which I was never going to do since I had just practiced a truth spell, she said, "Wait a minute. This is a tea to elicit the truth, isn't it?"

I could flail about with half-truths all I liked, but I'd done a great deal of work to make the space clear and clean and all about truth. Instead of answering her question, I went with one of my own. "I thought I was the first person to see Declan O'Connor dead in my shop. But you'd been there before me, hadn't you?"

Normally, I am such a people pleaser that it would be very difficult for me to confront someone like that. But I knew how important this was. Sure, I could have passed on what I knew to the Gardaí. It was quite possible that Kathleen had killed that man. But she was one of my sisters, and I couldn't do that to her. So I poured her a truth tea and decided to find out what I could myself.

"What on earth makes you ask me such a thing?" she blustered. Her cheeks grew ruddy, whether in anger or a blush of embarrassment, I couldn't yet tell. She hadn't drunk enough of my truth tea that it would make her spill her guts, but the fact that she must know I hadn't asked this question idly put her in a difficult position. Was she going to lie to me? Lie to one of her sisters?

Would she try and bluff her way out of this?

Finally, I could see when she made up her mind. She

pushed the tea away. "For heaven's sake, Quinn, get rid of this awful brew and bring me a proper cup of tea. I've been on my feet all day, and I'm parched. When I have a proper cup of Irish tea in front of me, I'll tell you everything."

I wasn't sure whether I should believe her. If I left her here, would she bolt out the door? Attack me in the kitchen?

Well, I'd asked her here for tea. At the very least, I could make her a proper cup of tea. It had been a while since I'd made my truth tea, and I'd forgotten how unpleasant it tasted. I had needed a whole lot more camouflaging herbs and sweeteners before it would be palatable.

And so I went into the kitchen and brewed us a fresh pot of tea. I even used a different teapot, being a bit worried that the bitterness of that root had penetrated the china. This was a bright chintzware pattern. I got out fresh teacups and added milk to the tray this time. I went in and found her standing, staring out the window. The sea was choppy and gray today. Perhaps it helped her focus as that candle had helped me.

I poured her the tea and she came and sat down again, almost without thinking added milk and sugar, stirred it, and took a couple of sips before she put it down and then turned to me. "Why would you ask me about the day of the murder like that? What is it you're accusing me of?"

Instead of sitting beside her, I chose the seat opposite so I could watch her face and read her expressions more easily."I'm not accusing you of anything. I only want the truth. I know you were there that night before I was." I took a sip of my own tea, as much for the hit of caffeine as for something to do with my hands.

She turned back, and I thought she looked paler than

when she'd come in. "Your magic must be stronger than I realized."

I shook my head. I went to the little dish on top of the mantelpiece and pulled out the button. I put it on the table in front of her. She picked it up, shook it around in her palm. "A mother-of-pearl button? There are thousands and thousands of these all over Ireland. What's that got to do with anything?"

"That green sweater you were wearing when I first arrived. I remember noticing the mother-of-pearl buttons and that they were all done up. Then, later on, when I'd found the body and you arrived, you were wearing a coat and dress."

"You take an awfully keen interest in my wardrobe."

I wasn't about to be sidetracked. "And the next time I saw that sweater, you'd changed the buttons."

She shrugged. "I was bored of the old ones. The shamrocks made me laugh."

They hadn't brought her luck, though. "Are we really going to play this game? I know you were there." Okay, I didn't really know she was there. All I knew was that this button seemed like pretty suggestive evidence to me. "Between the time you drove me to my cottage, when you had all your buttons, and the next time I saw you in that sweater, you'd lost one. And a button very much like your missing one turned up in my shop."

She looked at it again, shaking it in her palm as though it were a pair of dice and she might be a gambler. "Where exactly did you find it?"

"Very near the body. The forensics team only missed it because it had slipped between the floorboards."

She put the button down on the table so it made a tiny snap. "I see."

"Kathleen, I have to ask you. Did you kill Declan O'Connor?"

Her color fluctuated between bright, rosy red and deathly pale. She sipped her tea again, and this time I could tell that her hand was shaking. "No. I didn't kill Declan. I wouldn't."

"But you were very friendly with him, weren't you?"

She let out a great sigh. "I was. He was a charmer, that one. Never one you could take seriously or tie down. But it's a lonely life being different. For a few hours, he gave me the fantasy that I belonged."

Well, if she hadn't killed him, then how did that button get there? I had a feeling she wanted to wander off down memory lane and probably didn't have a lot of people she could talk to about her dead lover. However, I really wasn't interested in that journey. I wanted facts. "How did that button get in my shop so near to the dead man?"

Yep, that effectively pulled her back out of her reveries. "All right. I did go into the shop. I meant no harm, Quinn. My only intention was to walk around and make sure Lucinda had left things nicely for you."

"How did you get in?"

"I had a key."

"This doesn't make sense. Lucinda had already left the bookshop however she wanted it to be. What were you going to do? Dust the books?"

"I meant it as a gesture of friendship. That's all."

There was more, and I knew it. What was she keeping from me? She hadn't drunk much of my truth tea, but she'd drunk some of it. Besides, she was inside my magic circle.

This was a circle of truth. And I was determined to find hers.

She looked at me, but she wasn't so eager to chat anymore. I held her gaze, and then I had it. "You knew he'd be there, didn't you? Were you expecting to find him alive?"

Kathleen dropped her gaze, and I thought she was staring at that button, focusing the way I'd used that candle flame to focus. "He never met me there. But I had a feeling that he might have been taking advantage of Lucinda's absence. I wanted to make sure there was nothing you might find that would be upsetting for you."

A wave of revulsion swept over me. "Are you telling me Declan O'Connor used The Blarney Tome like it was the No Tell Motel?"

"I'm sorry, Quinn. I didn't know that he was, but knowing there's a sofa bed upstairs, it seemed like the sort of thing he might do, knowing Lucinda was gone."

"So he wasn't meeting you there?" That was what I'd feared.

"No."

"Then you knew you weren't his only ..." I didn't know what the correct term was here.

She obviously understood what I meant. Shook her head. She was staring out to sea again, but I watched her profile. Her jaw was set as through ready to take a blow. "No. I knew I wasn't the only one." Her smile was reflected in the window. "He told me I was special. The woman he'd been looking for his whole life." She laughed softly. "A load of malarkey, but I didn't mind hearing it."

It sounded remarkably like what he'd told Rosie Higgins.

Only she'd believed him. "How did you know you weren't the only one?"

"I used my scrying mirror. Saw him with another woman."

"A lot of people might say that was a motive for murder," I said.

She turned to me now. "I wouldn't kill Declan. I would have preferred not having to share him, but I understood that was his way. Anyway, if I'd wanted him all to myself, there were lots of ways I could have accomplished it, as you well know."

She was right. One good love spell, and he'd have been all hers. "Why didn't you?"

"Truth? I didn't want a full-time man. So I put up with what I got. It was enough."

She put her teacup down, and I offered her another cup. She must be parched by now.

"Have you anything stronger?"

I opened a bottle of red wine and ended up cooking pasta for the two of us while she tossed a salad and we continued chatting. I believed her, and if she hadn't killed him, then she was once more an ally.

"What happened when you went in that night?"

Kathleen seemed to think about it while we sat together at the kitchen table and ate. "I walked in and turned on the lights. I'd no reason not to. And I heard something."

My arms got goosebumpy. "Did you hear him being killed?" How awful would that be?

"No. I thought at first it was coming from outside, the back entrance. But I think it was the killer leaving."

"You came that close to coming face-to-face with a killer!"

I gulped wine. I couldn't imagine how it would have ended if she'd walked in ten minutes sooner.

"I know. But I didn't then, of course. I ran upstairs and checked that all was in order, which it was. I don't think Declan had carnal relations in your sofa bed."

"Good."

"I came back down, and something drew me to look behind the cash desk. You know how it is."

I did. What some people called intuition was a little stronger in our kind. "And he was dead?"

"He was, poor man. Exactly as you found him. I sat beside him and said my goodbyes. I shed a few tears. That must be when I lost the button."

"And you didn't see anything else at all?"

She looked a bit sheepish. "I picked up a cork."

"A cork?"

She motioned to the one lying beside our open bottle. "A wine cork. It was on top of the cash desk."

I was appalled. "You took away evidence from a crime scene? That is every kind of illegal."

"I was thinking of Eileen and Liam, I suppose. He used to bring wine, you see, when he'd come to visit. Sometimes flowers or a little gift, but always the wine. I didn't want Eileen to be upset by it."

"Where is this cork?"

She very deliberately put down her knife and fork and excused herself. She went to her handbag, which was sitting on my kitchen counter, and dug inside it to retrieve the cork. Who carried a wine cork around with them in their purse? "You kept it as a souvenir."

"Foolish, I know. It wasn't even meant for me, but I wasn't

thinking straight." She also hadn't reported the death. She'd left me to find Declan O'Connor.

And crucial evidence hadn't made it into the investigation.

She handed me the cork and, since it had been kicking around in her purse, I doubted there was any hope of evidence left if there'd ever been any. It was a perfectly normal looking cork, though it had the name of the wine imprinted on the side. *Vino d'Amour.* Wine of love?

"Why didn't you report the death?"

"Because I was a coward. I didn't want anyone to find out." She put down her fork and sipped her wine. "This is my home. I was afraid that if anyone began looking into me too closely they might find secrets I'd prefer to keep hidden."

She didn't want her neighbors finding out she was a witch. I got that. But she didn't seem to mind throwing me under the bus.

"You need to tell the Guards and give them that cork."

"No. I can't. But you can. Tell them you found it on the floor, where you found the button. You'll be fine because they know you didn't kill Declan. You'd have no reason to."

I shook my head and she threatened to throw it away if I didn't take the thing. What could I do? I put it in a sandwich bag. "I'm not lying to the Guards," I warned her.

"You don't have to. Just keep my name out of it."

CHAPTER 22

The next morning, Cerridwen was having a wonderful time chasing a moth that had flown into the shop. She was young enough yet that her hunting was more gymnastic than successful. I didn't think the moth was in much danger, and she was enjoying the sport, throwing herself at the walls and climbing up the bookshelves.

I, meanwhile, was wondering if I'd done the right thing letting Kathleen talk me into telling the detectives that I'd found the cork. Her argument was that since she hadn't killed Declan it hardly mattered whether she'd found the cork or I had. I wasn't so sure.

I called DI Walsh and he picked up. I told him about the cork and he said to hang onto it until they were back in Ballydehag.

The door opened, heralding new arrivals, and I turned to see three new customers standing there.

Something about them made me take a quick step back. It was a man, tall, dark and handsome with a cool, arrogant gaze. He had dark hair and icy blue eyes. With him were two older women. One was movie-star glamorous with silver-white hair. The other one was a comfortable, grandmotherly sort. I hadn't seen them before, but from the prickling at the back of my neck, I suspected they might be members of Lochlan's book club. I was beginning to see the signs. Not just the slight paleness of the skin, but a certain sleekness and power not usually found in older, Irish women.

"Can I help you?" I asked in my best professional bookseller's tone.

The man came forward with his hand outstretched. Odd. "My name is Rafe Crosyer. I'm an antiquarian book expert."

I shook his hand and wondered what on earth he was doing here. The most antiquarian thing in this bookshop was probably some of the old Mills & Boons on one of the lower shelves in the romance section.

"Hello. I'm Quinn Callahan."

"And these are my associates. Agnes Bartlett and Sylvia Strand."

The two ladies wished me a good morning.

"Are you looking for something in particular?" From their voices, they were all English.

"Are you the owner?" the man asked me.

"No. I work here."

He nodded as though I'd given the correct answer. "I'd heard that the owner moved away, quite suddenly."

Maybe I was wrong. Maybe he wasn't a vampire but a witch. I didn't think anyone outside the craft knew about Lucinda's sudden disappearance and my sudden move. "Where did you hear that?" I asked him.

He shrugged elegant shoulders. "Word gets around in book circles."

I doubted that the circles of an antiquarian book seller and somebody who looked as posh and rich as he did had much to do with a little, country bookstore in Ireland. Unless there was some secret bookcase I didn't know about where Lucinda kept all her treasures.

I watched him glancing around and had to ask, "Have you been here before?"

"No. Never. It's charming."

The one named Agnes agreed. "Look at those floors. And the space is perfect."

The two ladies didn't seem very interested in books. Both of them were looking at the front window and speaking in soft voices. I was certain they said something about skeins of wool and knitting needles.

I didn't really know what was going on here, but somebody was confused. Possibly me.

Agnes turned to me again. "Do you knit, dear?"

"Knit? No. I tried to learn when I was young, but it was both frustrating and boring. I never tried again."

"She sounds like our Lucy," Sylvia said, looking at Agnes with a smile.

"I do have some knitting books, though, in the crafts section. I could show them to you."

Rafe walked across the shop and, to my surprise, Cerridwen abandoned moth hunting, climbed down from the top of a bookshelf and hopped right onto his shoulder. The jacket he was wearing had to be Savile Row. I squeaked in alarm. "I'm so sorry. Cerridwen," I called to her. But the tall, dark stranger didn't seem at all bothered. "I like cats," he said, letting her ride on his shoulder. It was so charming, I warmed to him.

"The square footage is good," he said to himself.

"Cerridwen?" Agnes said from behind me. "Your cat's name is Cerridwen?"

"That's right. It's Irish."

"Yes. I know. Keeper of the cauldron."

We stared at each other, both assessing the other. "That's right," I said. Was she a witch? I got the feeling she was wondering the same about me.

Rafe turned to me. "Is there any kind of a back room? A place where you could run classes?"

"Classes? Most people who come here already know how to read."

Oh. Writing classes. I wondered if anyone had ever thought about that before. Not that Ballydehag seemed to be teeming with writers, but you never knew. "There's a space upstairs where I run a book club."

"Excellent. I'd heard this shop might be available to rent. That's why we're here, to look the shop over."

I felt righteous indignation spurt right into my chest. "Lucinda said you could rent her store?" What was I, chopped liver? Hauled all the way from Seattle to look after a store, and now it was going to be rented out from under me? Then what would I do?

He shook his head, looking as puzzled as I was beginning to feel. "A friend of mine lives here. He's the one who told me."

This man was definitely not a witch. Pale, strong and gorgeous? "Would your friend by any chance be Lochlan Balfour?"

He nodded, looking relieved that I'd guessed. "That's right. We're on our way to visit him, in fact. We thought we'd take a look in at the shop first."

"Why would an antiquarian book expert want to run a little bookstore in Ireland?"

He looked amused at my question. "No. My business is mainly in Oxford. And London. With occasional trips to Paris and New York. It's not for me." He gestured with his head, and I turned to see the two women stretching a cloth measuring tape across the window.

"They want to run a bookshop?"

"No. A knitting shop. Well, knitting and crafts."

We didn't have a knitting shop here, that was for sure. But if they turned The Blarney Tome into a knitting shop, then what would happen to the books? And my job.

"I'm pretty sure that Lucinda doesn't want the store to be changed. She hired me to run a bookstore. And I'm renting her cottage from her."

It was true we didn't have a formal agreement, which I'd been grateful for when I first arrived here. Now I wondered if I should have asked for a year's lease so I could stay put for twelve months without being thrown out on my ear by three snooty vampires from Oxford.

"I'm terribly sorry. I fear there may have been a misunderstanding."

I really doubted that Lucinda wanted to get rid of all her books and rent an empty shop to three vampires who wanted to knit. I felt fairly confident that I was safe. At least for now.

Rafe's nostrils suddenly twitched, and he walked unerringly over to where I had found Declan O'Connor dead on the floor. He glanced down, knelt so Cerridwen was treated to a joy ride, lifted the area rug that I had put over the spot and then, rising, looked over at me. "What happened here?"

Could I tell him? I couldn't think of a single reason not to. It wasn't like Lochlan and everyone else in town didn't know. "A man was killed here."

"Unfortunate for you. Was it while you were running the shop?"

"I found him when I first walked in. Before I even started the job." When I related the fact, I found myself surprised I hadn't run screaming back to Seattle.

The two women nudged each other, and the glamorous one said to me, "Oh, what a pity. Has it put you off staying?"

How eager they were to chuck out the books and bring in their wools and needles and crochet hooks.

I thought about the question. Weirdly, the murder hadn't scared me away. If anything, the drama and puzzle of trying to work out who in this village might be a murderer kept me busy, I supposed because I'd never lived here before and I didn't know anyone. I was coming fresh to the murder. Other people had their preconceived notions about their neighbors and no doubt all kinds of theories about who had done this and why, but I had none of that. All I had to go on was what I had personally seen, what I'd heard, and what people said about each other. It was a bit like what the police had, really. And I had the added advantage of living here, where they had to drive back and forth in order to continue their investigations.

Rafe was looking around the shop and out the window. He said, "Has the murderer been arrested?"

I shook my head. "The Gardaí are still investigating."

The three of them perked up at that. Rafe said, "We have some experience of amateur sleuthing. We've been involved in solving one or two murders. Perhaps we could help?"

I couldn't imagine how two old lady vampires and one antiquarian book dealer vampire could help solve a murder in Ireland, but on the other hand, how did I think I, a witch from Seattle, was going to do the job? Well, the truth was, I didn't. I fully anticipated that the Irish detectives would solve this crime, although there was a certain glamour in thinking that I might be able to help.

"What could you do?" I asked them.

"Well, we could—"

"Rafe! I thought that was your car out front."

I looked up to find Lochlan walking in the door, looking delighted to see Rafe.

The two shook hands. They were so different and yet so similar. Light and dark. Both tall, well-built and each gorgeous in his own way. But Lochlan had that shock of blond hair and Rafe the very dark hair. In truth, they made a stunning pair. I said in a rather acid tone, "These people seemed to think The Blarney Tome might be available to be turned into a knitting shop."

Lochlan scratched the back of his head and looked embarrassed. "I'm sorry about that. I did try to get hold of you and prevent this visit but—"

"We've been traveling," Rafe said. "Quinn was telling us that there's been a murder." I think all of us looked at the spot where poor Declan had lain. "We have some experience in helping solve murders."

And that was it? They'd come all this way to look at a

shop, and now they were moving on to sleuthing? What an odd trio.

"I'd heard something about that," Lochlan said. He looked at me and said, "What if we convened a special meeting of the book club this evening? Perhaps we could invite these three as our special guests. We wouldn't talk about a book; we'd throw out ideas about the murder."

I didn't want to be rude, but how much help could three strangers be?

Agnes, the grandmotherly of the two older women, looked at me. "You're wondering how three strangers could possibly help solve a murder among people they don't know. In a place they've never been."

"You can read minds?" I asked her.

She chuckled. "No. Your face gave your thoughts away."

I really had to work on that poker face. "Well, I guess that is how I feel. I'd only just arrived when the murder happened. I'm still trying to figure out who's who in this town."

Lochlan said, "Now I've brought you to Ballydehag, if I can't offer you a shop to rent, I can at least offer you a juicy mystery to solve." He said it like he was offering a big treat. "We've got any number of book club members who've been involved in all sorts of things throughout the years. Between us all, we might be able to put together a pattern. Worth a try, don't you think?"

They all looked at me.

Well, it wasn't like I had anything better to do at ten o'clock at night in a village that seemed to roll up the sidewalks about nine. With a shrug, I said, "Why not?"

The three visiting vampires looked quite pleased. I

supposed it made their trip less of a waste of time. I did feel bad though. "I'm sorry the shop's not available. Did you have your heart set on a knitting shop here?"

I didn't want to gossip, but I wondered if the bakery might soon be available.

"No, no," they hastened to assure me. They were looking in Dublin and Edinburgh and various other places. Rafe and the glamorous vampire looked to the grandmotherly one. "It's me, you see, dear. I'm quite picky. I loved my knitting shop in Oxford. But I can't really be seen there anymore. My death was too recent and people still remember me. And so we all think it would be easier if I found a new location."

Lochlan assured her she was welcome to stay at the castle as long as she liked.

"You have got to meet Bartholomew Branson," I said to her. "He's a brand-new vampire, and all he wants to do is go out and meet people. He has no idea about staying hidden from view."

They all stared at me. "Bartholomew Branson? I thought he'd drowned."

I shook my head. "Lochlan will explain it all to you. It's way above my pay grade."

I guess they all understood my hint that they should probably get out of my shop before a real customer came in. One whose blood actually pumped warmth through their veins. Lochlan said, "Come to the house. We'll have a good catch-up." House. Ha. But I supposed "come to the castle" sounded a little grandiose even to the undead.

He turned back to me. "Quinn? We'll see you at ten o'clock tonight?"

"Wouldn't miss it."

CHAPTER 23

I had the rest of the day to think about how we might be able to use the accumulated experience and brainpower of these Irish and English vampires. If Rafe and the two ladies had amateur sleuthing skills, the evening might not be a big waste of time. At the very least, I could talk through some of the things that were bothering me. It was weird, but it didn't feel like gossip talking to Lochlan and the other vampires. I knew they didn't really mix with the villagers. And they were the last ones to gossip. Well, no doubt they gossiped among themselves about each other, but I really didn't think they were too worried about the very human and, probably to them, dull goings-on of a bunch of Irish villagers. The only thing interesting was the murder.

Maybe I could ask their opinion on what I should do with the cork now in my possession.

I didn't have the originals from those notes that had been pushed under my door, but naturally, I had taken photographs of both of them, and they were on my phone. I decided to print those out.

I kept thinking about that cork that Kathleen had found near Declan O'Connor's body. Had he been drinking? Wine wasn't the sort of thing that a person would drink by themselves, and it sounded like, from what Kathleen had told me, Declan enjoyed a glass of his favorite beverage with his special ladies.

I'd asked if he bought the wine at her grocery store, which seemed like a very crass thing to do, but she said no, he bought the wine from the pub. Classy guy.

If he'd been drinking wine in my shop, then where was the rest of it? The bottle and glasses?

Who would know whether the dead man had been drinking wine when he died? No doubt it had come out in the autopsy, but I had no access. Or did I?

I thought maybe it was time I paid a visit to the doctor. He'd invited me to come and see him if I was upset by the death. I'd take him up on his offer. I called ahead, and the woman who answered said he finished his surgery hours at five o'clock. That was unfortunate, as that was when I closed the bookshop. I didn't think it was fair to close early just so I could do some snooping, so I asked if he could make a special exception and see me at five-fifteen. The woman gave a great sigh as though it was the most huge imposition ever and then said she'd ask him. She came back quite quickly to the phone and said snippily, yes, he would see me at five-fifteen. "And make sure you're on time," which I was pretty sure wasn't a message from her boss but something she'd decided to add herself.

Fortunately, I didn't have any customers at the very end of the day, so I managed to close the shop at five minutes before five. I got on my bike and within a couple of minutes was winding down a beautiful country lane. Rhododendrons were bursting into show-offy bloom. I passed the Catholic church, St. Patrick's, its steeple standing straight and tall like a wagging finger reminding villagers to behave. Behind the church, I passed the graveyard and thought one day I would have to find time to explore it. Some of the gravestones looked ancient. An enormous yew tree, gnarly and thick of trunk, had branches reaching far over the graveyard as though sheltering the inhabitants from inclement weather. This was where I turned, according to Google Maps.

I pedaled on down a road so narrow that if a car came, I'd have to flatten myself and my bike against the ancient, crumbling stone wall that followed the road. I saw fields of sheep and cattle and a wonderful old stone cottage, clearly no longer inhabited, as the roof was missing. While I watched, a fat hen waddled out of the open door. Talk about romantic ruins. I rode on past pretty little cottages and a huge field and then a fairly substantial-looking stone house. This turned out to be the doctor's. I wheeled up and left my bike leaning against the front wall. There was a sign saying "Surgery this way." I followed the arrow round to the side door which had another sign on it announcing that this was the Surgery. I opened the door and walked in. There was a small reception area out front with a dozen chairs, a counter with a computer on it and, behind that, a wall of files. Presumably this was the lair of the scary woman who hadn't wanted me to come. I was glad she hadn't waited for me. On the other side of the reception was a corridor, and I could see a light on in the open door at the end of it. "Hello?" I called.

"Is that Quinn? Come on through." I recognized the doctor's voice. I walked through and found him sitting at a desk covered in papers. He had reading glasses perched on his nose. He wore a white shirt with the sleeves rolled up and no tie. Every inch the country doctor.

He looked tired, as though it had been a long day. But I had the feeling he usually looked like that. "Quinn. I'm glad you came. How are you making out?"

Not only was this man the doctor and apparently the coroner and the pathologist, but I got the feeling he was the local psychologist as well. "I'm all right," I said. "But I have to be honest with you. It was a terrible shock finding that man dead on my floor."

"Of course it was. Are you sleeping all right?"

"I have dreams."

He nodded. Waiting. Did he think I was going to lie back and tell him my dreams? Who did he think he was, Freud?

I said, "I think I'd feel better if I knew more. Like what killed Declan O'Connor."

He looked surprised at my question. "Do you really want to dwell on all of that?"

Yes. I did. I wanted all the details. "I think it would help me if I could understand how he died. I keep making up stories in my head every time I look down at that spot where I found him." This was actually true.

"His throat was slit." This was no longer a secret. Cause of death had been reported in the news.

"No wonder there was so much blood," I said, almost without thinking.

He nodded. I pictured again the body as I'd first seen it. "But there was blood on the back of his head."

"You're a careful observer. He was hit on the head first and stunned. He hit the counter on the way down. Once he'd fallen, whoever killed him didn't have a struggling man to worry about."

Oh, that was cold. "So it might have been someone weaker?"

"That's possible."

"Could it have been a woman?"

He suddenly looked rather suspicious. "Why are you really here?"

Crap. Subtle I was not. "I need to understand. It's hard to explain, but having that man die in my shop makes me want to ..."

"Find his killer?" He skewered me with those dark brown eyes. "Have you been spending too much time reading your mystery section? Are you fancying yourself a Miss Marple?"

"Miss Marple?" I sat up straight, feeling quite offended. "Miss Marple is an eighty-year-old spinster."

He clamped down a smile at my outburst. "I merely meant you're a female amateur sleuth in a small village. No other comparison." Oh, wow. He was right. In thirty-five years, if I wasn't careful, I would *be* Miss Marple, only not as smart. I was going to have to take up knitting.

"Doctor Milsom, was there any alcohol in his system?" This was the main reason I was here, and now that he'd busted me anyway, I might as well ask my question, and we could both get on with our evenings.

"Call me Drew. This is obviously not a proper clinic visit, is it?"

I shook my head. He was being straight with me, and I decided to return the courtesy.

"Alcohol. Why do you ask?"

Who was interviewing whom here? "I'm trying to work out what could have happened."

"You could have asked twenty questions I would have expected before asking about alcohol." He could look very stern when he wanted to. "Quinn, if there's something you know about this murder, you must tell the Guards."

"I really don't. Honestly, I just have an interest since the man was killed in my shop."

He was looking at me from under his brows, and his gaze was disconcertingly direct. "I'm not one for scaremongering, but please don't forget that whoever did this is still out there."

My heart started to bang against my ribcage. "You think I could be in danger?"

He spread his hands in a helpless gesture. "For all I know, we're all in danger."

I was skeptical. "One murder in a sleepy village like this is bad enough. You're not seriously suggesting there's a serial killer on the loose, are you?"

His mouth quirked up a little at that. "It would be unusual, I admit. But serial killers are unpredictable people, and they follow unpredictable patterns. Well, unpredictable to anyone but themselves. Besides, I know a little about crime. Once someone has taken that step, once they've crossed the line between what is considered acceptable, civilized behavior and they've gone to the dark side, if you like, well, let's just say the second murder is always much easier than the first."

That made a lot of sense. And using his math, the third was easier yet, and the fourth and so on. I didn't like this notion of a serial killer at work. I also noticed that by dragging the conversation into serial killer territory, he hadn't answered my question. Not that he was obliged to, but I had come all this way. "Did you determine the time of death?"

Now he really did look amused. "Quinn. You know I can't tell you that."

I felt quite huffy. "Look. The detectives are using the bookshop as their base of operations." I pointed my index finger up to his ceiling. "Upstairs above my shop? That's their interview room. I am completely involved in this case."

He looked quite concerned. "That's a very odd place for them to conduct their investigation."

I shrugged. "I think so too. So maybe I'm not officially a cop, but I'm part of this thing."

He looked as though he was debating with himself and then went back to his usual, cynical, world-weary expression. "You tell no one. And if I find out you've been blabbing, there will be trouble for both of us."

I was in a pickle. I knew I was going to be doing some blabbing. But not to anyone he knew about. I settled on, "I promise not to tell a living soul." Which handily allowed me to still tell the vampires whatever I discovered.

"Time of death was between six and eight p.m." I was there about nine. But the timing did coincide with what Kathleen had told me. She'd dropped in about ten after eight, she'd said.

"There wasn't any alcohol in his blood, but alcohol doesn't last particularly long. He could have had a beer at lunchtime."

Ding ding ding. I felt like I should get a prize for asking the right question. No alcohol in his blood, but the cork out of the bottle? "But if he'd had a drink, say some wine, right before he was killed, you would have found that out?"

"Oh, yes. He'd had dinner. Pork with broccoli and potatoes, if you must know. No wine."

I thanked him for his time, and he reminded me once again to be careful who I asked pointed questions to. I promised to take his warning to heart.

I got back on my bike and headed back to the village, my mind whirling.

Going back to the cottage seemed very dull. I was on a roll. I wanted to keep sleuthing. Also, I was hungry and didn't want to cook for myself.

I decided to do a little bit more sleuthing before I met with the book club that night. I took the cork that Kathleen had given me and walked into the pub. There weren't many people there this time of night. A couple were having dinner, and a group of four men were swapping stories over pints.

I went up to the bar, and the guy behind it gave me a cheerful greeting. He was young, with black hair, a black beard, and a tattoo of a snake going up his arm. "Welcome. You're the lady that runs the bookshop."

"I'm Quinn Callahan."

He held out his hand. "Sean O'Grady."

"O'Grady? But the pub's called O'Brien's."

"I know. It was called that when I bought it, and I thought having a new publican was enough change for the people of Ballydehag. A name change might have killed them all."

I chuckled. "It's nice to meet you."

"What can I get you? First one's on the house."

I hadn't planned to have a drink, but what was I doing at a pub if I wasn't going to imbibe? I pulled the cork out of my purse. "A friend recommended this. Do you serve it by the glass?" He looked at the printed words, "Vino d'Amour."

He shook his head. "No. I've got a bottle in the back though."

"Can I buy it to go?"

"Course you can. But I'll still buy you a drink now while you tell me all about yourself."

I agreed and asked for a glass of white wine and ordered the fish and chips that was tonight's special, according to the chalkboard. He poured my wine for me, then rang up my fish and chips. "So, Quinn Callahan. What brings you to a town like this? All the way from America."

I didn't really want to tell him my whole life story, obviously, so I gave him the very short version. The one where I was divorced, not feeling very challenged in my work and needing a change. Most people seemed able to understand the idea of somebody in midlife just wanting a change. He nodded. "That's how I ended up here. I was in Dublin and got sick of it. I wanted a slower pace of life."

"Exactly. Seattle is so busy. It's kind of a relief to be somewhere so quiet. Where everyone knows each other."

"If you don't mind practically falling over a dead man when you arrive at your place of work."

I grimaced. "There is that." I wondered if I was always going to be known as Quinn, the woman who fell over a dead body the first time she walked into her shop.

"You've got backbone, I'll give you that. Most people I know wouldn't have bothered unpacking and got the next flight out of here."

"I hope I'm made of tougher stuff than that. Anyway, Declan O'Connor was a stranger to me."

"Not to me."

Oh, thank you, Sean O'Grady, for that perfect opening.

I sipped my wine. "Did he spend much time in here?"

"Declan? In the pub? No more than anyone else. He played darts sometimes of a Saturday. He used to come in with his wife for a meal now and then." He seemed suddenly struck. "Funny. He liked that wine that you've asked for."

Finally I was getting somewhere. I tried not to look too eager. "Really?"

"Yes. He probably bought two or three bottles a week."

Imagine that. "Did many other people in town buy that wine?"

"I wouldn't have said so. It's not the most popular wine. In fact, it's funny you should ask for it. Apart from Declan, not many people bother with it. It's easier for them to buy some plonk down at the grocer's."

I immediately felt that I had impressed him by being a woman of such refinement that she preferred to buy her wine from the pub than the grocery store. I pretended to think. "I can't remember who recommended it to me. It was a woman."

He shook his head. "Can't help you there. Declan's mainly the one I remember buying it."

My fish and chips came up then, and between customers, Sean O'Grady chatted to me about his travels in and around Seattle. He was a hiker and a kayaker, and he'd moved to Cork for the outdoor pursuits. Cycling and hiking and even surfing. "You must try cycling the Wild Atlantic Way. Absolutely breathtaking." I enjoyed chatting about something other than murder and eating excellent fish and chips. I suspected I'd be back more often than was good for my waistline.

When I was finished, Sean went to the back to fetch my bottle. "Do you need a bag?"

I shook my head. "I'm only carrying it next door to the bookshop." I glanced at the label which was a cartoon image of two intertwining hearts. Subtle it was not.

"Don't let the label fool you. The wine's quite good."

Vino d'Amour? I suspected that Declan O'Connor hadn't chosen that wine for its citrus highlights and plum undertones. This was a guy who used wine to get laid.

CHAPTER 24

I had a couple of hours still until the meeting, so I went back to my cottage. I'd had dinner but Cerridwen hadn't and she wasn't a cat who liked to miss meals. I sat in the living room with tea and tried to pull together the evidence and my questions. I'd asked Lochlan to bring a whiteboard to tonight's meeting, assuming he'd have such things since he ran a multinational corporation from his castle.

There was a knock on my door. I went to the front door and peeked out the little window and saw Kathleen standing there, looking nervous. With her was the most astonishing-looking woman. She had long, flowing, silver-blond hair and a face that looked sort of the way Renaissance painters used to paint the Virgin Mary, round with big, pure, blue eyes and, let's face it, a slightly smug expression. She had managed to give birth to Jesus, after all.

I was honestly tempted to ignore these visitors who hadn't bothered to tell me they were coming, since I was trying to prepare for the book club meeting, but they were witches, and there was no hiding from them. I pasted a pleasant expression on my face and opened my door. "Kathleen? What a surprise."

She immediately launched into a fast and slightly apologetic explanation. "I'm so pleased you're home, dear. I've had a surprise visit from the head of our coven, Pendress Kennedy."

Pendress of the flowing silver hair gave me a nod and walked right into my home. I wasn't sure at all what to make of her. Kathleen made a helpless expression and half rolled her eyes while the other woman had her back turned and then followed her inside.

"This is a sweet cottage." Pendress drew in a deep breath, closed her eyes and then let it out again. "Yes. A very good atmosphere. I see you've been cleansing your space. That's a good idea, considering."

Considering what? Pendress was wearing a blue velvet dress that flowed like a royal robe around her. When she moved her hands, silver bangles sounded like musical chimes on her wrists. She had dangling moonstone earrings and a necklace featuring moonstone, pink quartz and obsidian.

"I wanted to stop in and see how you're getting on," she said. The words were pleasant enough, but I thought there was a sharp warning in those placid, blue eyes.

"I'm settling fine, thank you." I wasn't sure if I should offer refreshment. Trouble was, I had places to be and people to meet two hours from now, and I didn't want my witch sisters to know.

She gestured to the candles on the mantelpiece. "Shall we have some light, my dear?"

I glanced between the two of them. Was she testing me?

"Of course." I turned to look at the candles. "Let there be light." The candles leapt into flame.

"Very nice."

Did she really think I needed praise for such a simple spell? "That's one of the first spells I ever learned."

"And later you learned some rather more complicated spells, I understand. You set yourself up against death. And for a while, you held the dark foe at bay."

I crumpled to the couch like a piece of cardboard that someone had crushed in their hands. "I'm so sorry about that. You don't know how I regret it."

"You've plenty of time to make amends."

Since she was the head of my coven, and nobody got that job without being a very powerful witch, I asked the question that had been burning on my mind. "Pendress, do you think me wrongly extending my ex-husband's life is what caused Declan O'Connor's murder?"

She seemed a little taken aback by the question. "You do take rather a lot onto yourself. Why would you think such a thing?"

I felt certain she knew and only wanted me to repeat myself out loud. I obliged her. "It's the butterfly effect, isn't it? I tampered with fate. How can I be sure that pulling my husband back from death didn't somehow, all these miles away, push Declan O'Connor toward it?"

"First of all, that's an arrogant presumption. I hear you're quite a good witch, but that would take powers even I don't possess." She obviously saw my distress and smiled kindly at me. "Unless you murdered that man with your bare hands, you are not responsible for his death."

I didn't know if she was telling the truth or even if she

knew, but still her words brought me an enormous sense of relief. "Are you certain?"

"Yes, dear. I'm certain. However, what you did was still wrong, and if I hear of any further ..." She seemed to search for the correct word and came up with, "antics, then we will be forced to consider further actions. Do I make myself clear?"

"Yes."

"Good. We'll look forward to welcoming you to the coven at our next meeting."

I glanced at Kathleen in alarm. I wasn't ready to face a coven of witches, all of whom knew I had meddled where I shouldn't. "But I'm so busy here."

Her laugh was musical and tinkling and yet still not a pleasant sound. "You're much less busy than when you actually had friends and a full life and a more demanding job back in Seattle." She glanced around. Through the window was darkness where only the sound of the ocean gave any inkling that it was even there. The castle had only a few lights on, so it looked more like a lighthouse on a desolate peninsula. "This hardly seems like a bustling metropolis."

Okay, she had me there. "Still, I'd feel so uncomfortable. Couldn't I wait a couple of months until I feel more settled? Until the other witches have had time to forget the mistake I made?"

She grew quite firm. "You will turn up at the coven meeting because I have requested you to. Do you understand?"

It wasn't a request. It was an order, and we both knew it. I didn't know what they would do if I didn't, but based on the fact that I was now living on the other side of the world from where I'd begun, I didn't really want to test her. I nodded silently.

"Very well," Pendress said.

"The Gardaí want to speak to Lucinda." I'd told Kathleen already and wasn't surprised when Pendress nodded. "I have arranged it. You will not get involved, if you please."

"Why can't I speak to her? I'm running her shop. I have questions." What was the big deal?

She shook her head, and that wonderful hair shimmered in the candlelight. "It's out of the question." Before I could argue, she said, "Cerridwen. What a pleasure to see you back home."

She knelt and the black cat came forward and bowed her head, then looked up to gaze into Pendress Kennedy's eyes. "You're looking after Quinn, I can see that. And you've only to come to me if you need my help."

Cerridwen nodded her head up and down. Typical cat behavior, of course, but it really did look like she was nodding in agreement.

Pendress rose. "I really came for some Mandrake root. Lucinda's an excellent herbalist. I do hope you'll keep up her garden?"

"I'll try." I was a reasonable gardener, but this country was new to me, as was the soil and growing conditions. I didn't want to be responsible if something went wrong. "I saw some in the garden shed. I'll get it for you."

She held up a hand. "Don't trouble yourself. I know my way around. Good night, sister. Blessed be."

"Blessed be," I replied, more grateful that this frightening witch was leaving than irritated that she wouldn't let me contact Lucinda Corrigan.

THERE WAS a palpable sense of excitement when I walked upstairs in my bookshop. I could tell even as I put my foot on the first rung of the spiral staircase that there were already creatures up above me. It was five minutes before ten. They must be eager. Lochlan hadn't bothered to return my key. I doubted vampires needed such mundane things as keys, anyway.

I climbed to the top and walked in and was quite surprised by what I saw. The normal members of the book club were there and chatting away like old friends to Rafe and Sylvia and Agnes. The promised whiteboard was in place with a fresh box of markers.

Amid all the chatter, Lochlan Balfour glanced up when I arrived. It was as though he had sensed me there. I wasn't sure how comfortable it made me to be so easily on the radar of a vampire. He rose and swiftly crossed the room to me. "The whiteboard was a good idea. In fact, I'll give you this one. Might come in handy when discussing books."

"That looks like something the cops would use," I said.

"Exactly."

Already taped to the board were the pictures that I had received showing Rosie Higgins and Karen Tate with Declan O'Connor. I was puzzled. "Where did you get those? Do you have a contact in the police?"

"No. I got them off your phone."

"You guessed my password?"

The look he gave me was somewhat condescending. "I didn't have to."

"Have you heard of privacy laws?" I really didn't know why I bothered.

He merely shook his head at me. "I've always believed that rules were meant to be broken."

Note to self: Take anything personal off my phone. The sad thing was, there wasn't anything racy or exciting. Note to self: Don't bother.

I'd talk to him later about personal boundaries, but for now, I was quite excited to get the sleuthing started.

Rafe was holding forth about some murder or other he'd somehow been involved with, and then he saw me too. He graciously gestured for me to come forward. "Quinn. This is your shop. Why don't you take over?"

He handed me an erasable pen for the whiteboard as though he were handing me a sword and asking me to lead them into battle. I felt embarrassed that they were deferring to me. What did I know about sleuthing?

When I hesitated, Bartholomew Branson rose to his feet and took a step forward. "Perhaps I could—"

Suddenly, I was as powerful as any police chief in the world. "That's okay, thanks. I've got it."

I strode with a confidence I was far from feeling up to the whiteboard. I tried to remember the last crime show I'd watched on television or the last police procedural novel I'd read. Okay, think. What did sleuths do? They looked for suspects, clues, motives. I wrote each of those words along the top of the board and underlined it. "Okay, what do we have?"

Agnes Bartlett pointed to the two grainy photographs that had been printed out. "I'd say those two were suspects."

"Good. Right."

I wrote down Rosie Higgins and Karen Tate under Suspects. And so much for my pleasure at discovering a nice singleton friend if Karen turned out to be the murderer.

"What do we know about these two suspects?" I knew a little, but the vampires had been here a lot longer. I didn't know how much they mingled with regular people, but maybe they knew more than I did.

However, there was silence.

Okay, moving on. "Someone, and we don't know who, snapped these photographs of Declan O'Connor, our murder victim, with both the butcher's wife and Karen Tate, the woman who runs Granny's Drawers. It appears that he was having intimate relations with both of these women."

I wrote Photographer? on the edge of the board and circled it.

"Supposition or fact that your victim was having affairs with both of those women?" Rafe Crosyer asked.

I was pleased that he was questioning everything. "The butcher's wife, Rosie Higgins, admitted it to me. Also, I believe she confessed it to the police. Karen Tate, the woman who runs Granny's Drawers, didn't admit anything to me, but two elderly ladies said they'd seen Declan O'Connor spending time with her. One of the two was quite suspicious."

"I understand the vic's throat was slit," Bartholomew Branson piped up. "If the butcher suspected his wife, well, in my novel *Fatal Vow,* the main suspect was also a jealous husband and in chapter three—"

"Thank you, Bartholomew," Lochlan said, cutting him off. "Excellent suggestion. Obviously, if Sean Higgins discovered that Declan O'Connor was having it off with his wife, that would be a pretty sound motive for murder."

I wrote down Sean Higgins, butcher, as the third suspect. The police had already interviewed him about the murder. They must not have enough evidence yet, as there'd been no arrest.

"What are their alibis?" This was Sylvia, the glamorous vampire. She looked like someone on TV playing a detective.

A fluttery woman who'd been sitting at the back suddenly said, "I thought it was you. But until I heard your voice, I wasn't certain. Sylvia Strand, I adored your pictures. Oh, that movie you made with Rudolph Valentino. I believe it changed the course of my life. I'm Connie," she said at last, as though she might ask for an autograph.

The glamorous woman looked quite pleased and not particularly surprised at the adulation. She gave a coy glance. "Which of the movies that I made with Valentino might you be referring to, my dear?"

Oh, she was good. Connie lost even more of her poise. "They were all wonderful. But my favorite was *The Renegade.* You were so beautiful. And Valentino. He was so ..."

"Difficult to work with," Sylvia snapped. She paused for a moment, and then her faced softened. "But quite as good-looking up close as on the screen. And he had a personal magnetism I've rarely seen since."

The woman's hand flew to her chest. "Was it true then? Were you? More than just good friends?"

You could have heard a pin drop. Everyone was fascinated by a drama that must have taken place a hundred years ago. Sylvia turned her head in a way that I bet she'd done in her acting days. "My dear, a woman never tells." Then she gave a soft chuckle. "But I do have a very nice set of rubies in my safe. Given to me by a very special man."

Then she turned back. "But we're getting sidetracked. Please, Quinn, carry on. We were discussing alibis."

Oh man, how was I going to keep their attention after that? She'd had an affair with Rudolph Valentino, and I had the only eligible man in my age group comparing me to an eighty-year-old spinster who spent her spare time knitting.

Right, I should have had a column for alibis. Darn. I was such an amateur. Still, I refused to be beaten so quickly in the game. "Right. I was able to discover that time of death was between six and eight p.m. I don't know what their alibis are," I admitted.

"Can we find out?" she asked Rafe. Who looked at Lochlan. "You must have contacts in the Guards?"

He nodded. "I took the liberty." He reached for a file folder and opened it. "Rosie Higgins says she was having dinner with her husband, Sean Higgins. They ate at half past six and after dinner they watched television. They were never out of each other's sight."

"So the wife alibis the husband and vice versa," Sylvia said. She made a face. "Weak."

"And Karen Tate was on a Skype call with her sister in Sweden between six and seven p.m., which has been confirmed. Afterward, she says she took a bath. She lives alone and no one can verify."

"Also weak," Sylvia said.

I still couldn't get over that they had access to police files. It was like hanging out with a bunch of secret agents. Or superheroes.

I just hoped they were the good guys.

CHAPTER 25

"There's something else you need to know," I said. I didn't relish sharing what I'd learned about Kathleen, mainly because I didn't think she had had anything to do with the murder, but it was important that they have the whole picture. I told them about the button and the sweater and that she had withheld evidence. I pulled out the cork and laid it on the table where normally the book club would lay their notes or copies of the novel we were reading. It sat there looking sad and forlorn, a little lonely cork bobbing about in the ocean.

"And the significance of this is?" Balfour asked.

"According to Kathleen, this was the cork from a bottle of the type of wine that Declan always brought when they spent time together." I brought out the bottle that I had bought that day and showed them the label.

Both Lochlan and Rafe looked horrified. "*Vino d'Amour*? One word in Spanish, or Italian I suppose, and one in French? I wouldn't expect much." Rafe said, and Lochlan agreed. "And the cork was in the shop with the dead man?"

"Yes. She took the cork away. She came in before I arrived that night and found Declan O'Connor dead on the floor. She says she heard someone leaving out the back. But by the time she got to the back door, they were gone. She came back and saw that cork lying on the counter. Because it was so associated with her time with Declan, she picked it up and put it in her handbag. And then she left and locked the front door behind her."

Lochlan looked quite annoyed. "You're saying that woman could have spared you the shock of finding a dead body in your shop on your very first day in this town and instead she kept her mouth shut?"

Yep, pretty much. I simply nodded.

She was the closest thing to a friend I had in this village, and the way Lochlan was looking at me, I didn't feel like I had the most reliable one. It was really a case of beggars and choosers.

"You have to add her name to the list of suspects," Lochlan said. There was general nodding and murmurs of agreement.

I hated to do it, but I could see they were right. I only had Kathleen's word for it that she'd stumbled on the man when he was already dead, and she hadn't admitted it until I'd confronted her.

Oscar Wilde, who'd seemed to be snoozing so far, said, "He had good stamina for a mortal, I'll give him that. We know that Declan O'Connor was seeing not one but three shopkeepers. One wonders he could tell them apart."

"Don't be such a snob, Oscar," Lady Cork said. "A shopkeeper has as much right to romance as anyone."

"And I think that's what Declan gave them," I agreed. "All

the women said he made them feel special. I think only Kathleen knew she wasn't his only love."

"So the women didn't know about each other?" Deirdre asked.

"Well, whoever took these pictures knew about them," Oscar reminded her. "It's so sordid, I quite long to meet the photographer."

"And yet Kathleen McGinnis's picture isn't included," Sylvia reminded us. "Might she be the photographer?"

"Motives," I said, tapping my barely used pen against the word.

"Jealousy? Revenge?" Lady Cork offered.

"Rosie Higgins swore to me that she didn't kill Declan O'Connor. She said they were in love and he was planning to leave his wife for her. Why would you kill the man you were planning to marry?"

"Perhaps she found out about her rivals?" Lady Cork suggested.

I wrote Jealousy and Betrayal under motive.

I wasn't actively trying to throw the blame away from Kathleen, but there was another, far more likely suspect if jealousy was the motive. "What about Declan O'Connor's wife? If he was planning to leave her for Rosie Higgins, might she kill him?"

"She might, of course. I've always thought the baker's wife to be a rather pragmatic, easygoing sort of woman. If you ask me, the love of her life isn't the husband but the son," Lochlan said. "Still, put her name on the board. Why not?"

So I did. And for motive, I had the same. Those kissing cousins Betrayal and Jealousy.

We all looked at the board, and no one had anything more to offer. "Are we stuck?" Agnes Bartlett asked.

I stared at the board and nodded. "We don't know enough. I suppose I could do what I did with Kathleen. I make a tea that encourages people to tell the truth. Perhaps I need to invite each of our suspects over for tea."

"Too dangerous," Lochlan said immediately. "If you confront the killer and you begin asking pointed questions, you may find yourself at the wrong end of a knife."

My hand slipped to my throat instinctively as though I could protect it. "Okay, I won't tackle them in my cottage. But how else do we find out more about these women?"

There was a silence, and then suddenly Lochlan said, "Naturally, it will be at the party welcoming you to Ballydehag."

"Party? What party?" I hadn't heard of any welcoming do. In spite of the darkness of tonight's events, I was flattered. Already running through my wardrobe for an appropriate outfit.

Lochlan Balfour continued, "The party that I shall hold at the castle. We'll make sure everybody who could possibly be a suspect, or who might know anything about the crime, is invited."

Oh. I went from flattered to crushed. There was no party to welcome me to town, merely a ruse to sniff out a killer. Still, it was a good idea, I had to admit.

"But will they all come?" Agnes Bartlett asked.

Lochlan looked at her as though she'd asked a very stupid question. "The people of this village have been dying to get a look inside my castle ever since I bought it. Oh yes, they'll come."

He was so cool and arrogant that I half-wished they'd turn him down on principle. Though I suspected he was right. If the other residents of Ballydehag were like me, they'd be thrilled to get inside that castle and have a poke around. I wondered if there were dungeons. Perhaps ghosts. Or were ghosts frightened away by vampires the way most people were frightened away by ghosts?

"Saturday night, I think," he said. So coolly arrogant, as though all the world would drop everything because he said so.

"Saturday night? That's only three days away. What if I have plans?"

He could barely suppress the amusement in his eyes. "Do you have plans?"

"Nothing I can't change," I said with what dignity I could muster.

"I have an excellent caterer, if you need one," Rafe said.

"Thank you. But unnecessary. I like to give my business to the locals. We'll have Sean O'Grady, the young man who runs the pub, do the catering."

I thought that was a stunningly smart idea. Not only would Sean O'Grady appreciate the business, but he was also the man who supplied Declan's wine.

"We should get him to serve *Vino d'Amour* at the party."

"Good idea, Quinn," Oscar drawled. "Though the way it was getting about, it seems that *Vino d'Amour* has loose standards. Rather like me."

We ended the evening with Lochlan planning to invite everyone who could possibly be involved in Declan O'Connor's murder to my welcome party.

Bartholomew rubbed his hands together. "It's been too

long since I was at a party. I'm very good at reading people and decoding their body language. Comes of being an international bestselling novelist."

Everyone turned in alarm, but it was Oscar who gently said, "You and I, my dear Bartholomew, will be confined to quarters. The downside of being a recognizable literary figure is that one can't show oneself to one's adoring public." He paused, glanced over at Bartholomew and said, silkily, "I've had to cope with post-mortem fame for one hundred and twenty years. I expect your sentence will be much shorter."

Before Bartholomew had worked out that he was being insulted, Lochlan quickly ended the meeting.

Everyone left, and when I'd turned out the lights, I found Lochlan waiting for me downstairs. "Did you forget something?" I asked.

"No. I wanted to make certain you got home all right."

"Oh." I didn't know whether to be offended at his overprotectiveness or flattered.

CHAPTER 26

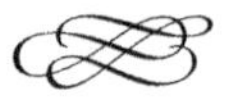

"Good morning, Mrs. O'Leary," I said as the local schoolteacher walked into my shop the next morning.

"Good morning, Quinn."

I was beginning to feel like I was fitting in here. I knew people's names, and they knew mine.

She glanced around. "Where's Cerridwen this morning?"

Cerridwen had taken a great shine to Mrs. O'Leary. Mostly because the woman usually had a little cat treat in her pocket. She'd explained that she couldn't have a cat of her own since her husband was allergic, so it was a great treat for her to come here and sit in one of the chintz armchairs reading a book, my cat happily curled up in her lap. But today, Cerridwen was acting peculiar.

"I don't know what's wrong with Cerridwen today." In fact, I suspected there was a mouse behind one of the bookshelves, for Cerridwen had run down one of the aisles earlier and then stopped. She was sitting in the middle of the floor looking intently at one of the bookshelves. Her tail twitching on the floor was the only movement.

"I'll see if I can rouse her," Mrs. O'Leary said. We both walked to the travel section, and sure enough, there was Cerridwen sitting exactly where she'd been for the last hour.

"Good morning, my sweet love," the teacher cooed. Cerridwen looked over but didn't come running up as she usually would.

"You're being coy, are you? What do you think I've got in my pocket?" She walked forward, holding out the cat treat. Cerridwen looked quite pleased to see her coming and daintily took the offered treat, but still she didn't move.

"Perhaps there's a mouse behind that bookcase," Mrs. O'Leary said. It was what I'd thought too, but I didn't really want to be advertising that I had a vermin problem in the bookstore. In fact, I hadn't known until now that there was one.

"Maybe."

The woman's eyes twinkled when she looked at me. "Or maybe she's planning a trip. She's got her eye on Bali, I see."

We both laughed, and then she told me why she was really there. She wanted to order some books for one of her classes. It was an easy enough thing for me to do, and then with a final goodbye to Cerridwen, she left.

I walked back toward the travel section. "You're not exactly pulling in the business, you know. We don't want people to get the idea there are mice in here."

Cerridwen looked at me and her tail flicked again.

"What is it, you funny thing?" I asked her. I picked her up. She was usually game for a cuddle, but she made an annoyed sound and struggled to get down.

"You're going to make me move this bookcase, aren't you? And if there's a mouse behind it, it's just going to run away again."

I was wondering if I should invest in a mousetrap when Lochlan walked in. Cerridwen wouldn't leave her spot, not even for him.

"Good morning," I said to the vampire who never seemed to sleep, neither day nor night. "What brings you into my bookstore so early?"

"I wanted to go over the guest list to your party."

I made a sound like Cerridwen had when I'd picked her up against her will. "My party? As if. I'm only an excuse to lure a murderer."

He looked slightly taken aback. "I suppose you're right." He paused to think. "I meant no disrespect. May I make it up to you? After?"

Now I felt like a jerk. "No. You don't have to. I'm only teasing."

"I'd like to."

"You're going to order more *Vino d'Amour* and sausage rolls?"

"Please. I've got some very nice vintage champagne in my cellar. I'll fly in a chef or take you to any restaurant you fancy. The Guy Savoy is nice."

"Guy Savoy? That sounds French."

"Yes. It's in Paris."

"You want to take me to Paris for dinner?"

He shrugged. "It's close, and the food's excellent. But if you prefer London or New York, say the word."

"Maybe we should get through this weekend first," I said, feeling a bit faint. I was not the kind of woman who was whisked away to Paris for dinner. Or I never had been.

He gave me the guest list to peruse and, while I was doing it, wandered off to look at the new books that had arrived.

I checked out the list, and everyone I could think of was on it and quite a few I'd never heard of and had yet to meet. I heard him say, "And good morning to you, Miss Cerridwen."

I followed to tell him his list looked fine and to see if she'd move for Lochlan, but she only stared at him with her green-gold eyes, remaining fixed in her spot.

"I think there might be a mouse behind that bookshelf. She will not move."

Lochlan looked down at me with a quizzical expression. "You're not mistaking me for an exterminator, are you?"

"No. Just wondering if I should get a trap."

"I'd leave Cerridwen to do what she does best," he said.

"I know, but it would be horrible if I had customers in here and my cat was racing around after a mouse." It sounded like something you'd see in a cartoon.

He walked toward Cerridwen and leaned down to give her a pat. Then slowly, he rose again.

I could see his nostrils twitching, and I had to ask. "What is it?"

"There's a scent I recognize."

"Of mouse?"

He shook his head. He went closer to the books. He was like a nearsighted person trying to read the book spines. I came up beside him. For some reason, the hairs on the back of my neck had started to rise. There was a section, not a particularly large section, on sights to see in the British Isles. A couple of the books seemed to have been pushed out of position somehow. Lochlan pulled two of them away, and a cry escaped me.

"Not a mouse," he said.

We both looked at the space behind where the books had been. There was a knife in there. A knife with a stained blade. I said, "Is that what I think it is?"

"If you're thinking that might be the missing murder weapon, I'd say you're in the right of it."

"Couldn't it just be a prank? A cruel joke? That could be any kind of blood on the knife."

He shook his head. "It's Declan O'Connor's."

"How can you be so sure?"

He tapped the side of his nose. "Nose of a bloodhound." Cerridwen made a *brrp* sound, and he looked down at her. "Beg your pardon. Or cat."

I gulped and stepped back until my back bumped the bookshelf behind me.

"Why me?" I asked nobody in particular.

"It's not you. This is all part of a pattern."

"Maybe the killer panicked. Shoved that knife behind some books knowing it would be ages until I found it. I mean, how many people come in here looking for travel guides to the British Isles?"

"You'd best call the guards. And don't touch the knife."

What was I going to do? I had customers. "I can't have people wandering in here looking for the latest romance or thriller when I've got a murder weapon in the middle of my travel section."

"Good thing it wasn't in the mystery section," he said.

I winced. He said, "Put up your 'gone for lunch' sign."

"There's a 'gone for lunch' sign?"

"If there isn't, you'd best make one right now. Get a scrap of paper, write out 'closed for lunch' and tape it to the front door."

I was acting like a blithering idiot. He was right, of course. He carried the books carefully and put them on the desk beside the cash register.

I found my hands were shaking as I once again put in a call to the Gardaí. While I was doing that, Lochlan rummaged around behind me and found my order book. He ripped out a page from near the back and, taking a Sharpie from the drawer beneath my cash desk, wrote 'Closed for a break. Back shortly.' He found my Scotch tape and affixed the sign to the front door. While he was doing that, I spoke to the inspector. I told him what I'd found, and he said not to touch anything, obviously, and he was on his way. The bloodstained knife definitely got more interest than a stray wine cork. I'd tucked the white board away in the upstairs closet, but I'd have to make sure there wasn't anything else up there I didn't want the detectives to see.

"Are you all right?" Lochlan asked me. He put his hands on my shoulders. They were pleasantly cool, considering how overheated I felt. I nodded. "It's just that it brings it all back again. I'm barely over the shock of finding that dead man in my store, and now I'm faced with the knife that killed him? Could they not have thrown it somewhere else?"

"It is odd. All the ways you can dispose of a murder weapon. Why would the killer leave it somewhere where it was bound to be found? Or maybe, as you said, they just panicked."

Or the worst maybe of all, what if it hadn't been there on

the night of the murder? What if someone had planted it in my shop?

And why?

"Do you know what kind of knife that is?" I asked.

"It looks to me like a butcher's knife."

CHAPTER 27

When the priest walked into my bookshop later that day, I immediately scanned my conscience for things I might have done wrong. Priests had that effect on me, in the same way that if I saw a police officer, I immediately thought I was about to be arrested for some crime I didn't even remember committing. However, the man wearing the priest's collar looked benign and friendly. He walked right up to me, not even bothering to browse the books first. "Good afternoon. I'm Father O'Flanagan. I've been meaning to get by, but it's been busy. I wanted to come along and say hello."

Oh dear, was he trolling for more bodies in pews? I said, "Good afternoon." Then we stood there staring at each other for a second. Oh, right, I should introduce myself. "I'm Quinn Callahan." And I didn't know what else to say, so I added, "I'm sorry to say, I'm not a Catholic."

He chuckled, a low, rich tone. "That's all right. I'm here for your books, not your soul."

It was such an unexpected line from a priest that I burst out laughing. "Well, that's good. I have plenty of books."

"I'm in need of a good gardening book. I've got some sort of a blight on my roses. It's not the aphids, and it's not black spot. I'm not entirely sure what it is or what to do about it. I know Lucinda used to have quite a good gardening section."

"I'm not sure how good it is, but I can take you to the books we have."

"I'm usually in to get the Brother Cadfael mysteries. Do you know them?"

Of course I did. They were mysteries about a priest, set in the Middle Ages, I thought. "Aren't they a bit close to home for you?"

He shrugged. "It's nice to see a man of the cloth being allowed to use his brain and solve murders. Not that writing sermons isn't tiring work, but sometimes it would be nice to get out and get one's hands dirty, as it were."

"Well, the gardening must help with that."

It was his turn to chuckle. "It does that."

I said, "Well, if you're looking for a murder mystery to solve, unfortunately we have one right here in Ballydehag."

He shook his head, looking quite concerned. "Declan O'Connor wasn't one to warm the pew every Sunday, but poor Eileen, now, she's a rock of the church. It's a terrible blow to her and their son."

I nodded. "Eileen said that she had been doing the flowers in the church when her husband was killed."

"She was, yes. A beautiful arrangement she made. The woman's got such a talent with flowers. It was a joy between confessions to come out and see the arrangement grow. I have an interest in flowers, but she's got a blessed green thumb."

"She grew the flowers that she put in a church flower arrangement?" If they were like when I'd been a kid, those arrangements were enormous. And the church I'd passed on my bicycle might not be as big as a cathedral, but it wasn't tiny. She must indeed have a green thumb.

"We haven't the money for fancy arrangements to be brought in, so we make do with what we have. Oh yes, we've got some wonderful gardeners and very creative minds. In the middle of winter, as you can imagine, it takes a bit more effort than this time of year."

"What a sad thing to think of her arranging flowers, so oblivious, while that terrible thing was happening to her husband."

"It may be a cliché, my dear, but the Lord does move in mysterious ways. Eileen's a strong woman blessed with a fine son. She'll get through this."

"Well, I'll leave you to it then. Let me know if there's anything else I can help you with."

"I wish you could encourage the author to write a new Brother Cadfael mystery, but sadly, she's passed on."

"That was sad." I'd enjoyed the series too.

While I worked at the cash desk, I wondered if a priest with an interest in murder mysteries might be of help. No doubt most of the people in this village went to confession. He must know everyone's secrets. But if I knew anything from what I'd read, the confessional was sacred. If he was a good priest, he'd never tell.

Rosie Higgins came in looking pale and as though she hadn't slept or combed her hair in some time. I hadn't seen her since DI Walsh removed the knife from my shop. I imagined as soon as they could confirm it was Sean Higgins's knife, they'd be back to arrest him. Did Rosie have an inkling of the trouble that was coming? "I need something to take my mind off the terrible loss," she said in a low, anxious tone. "Give me something light. Something that will make me laugh."

I thought if she was feeling bad now, she'd be feeling a world of hurt when her husband was arrested for murdering her lover. "Do you want something modern? Irish?"

"I don't care. So long as it's funny."

I led her to what I termed the chick lit section, but as she passed across the aisles, Father O'Flanagan called out, "Well, hello there, Rosie. And how are you getting on?"

"Oh, Father O'Flanagan. Fancy seeing you here. I've just come for something light to read. It's been such a terrible shock, losing a friend and neighbor like that."

"I know. Declan O'Connor's death has touched us all."

He came forward with a book on roses in his hand. He paid and then said to her, "I'll see you on Sunday."

"No, Father. You'll see me Saturday night. We're all invited to Devil's Keep."

"You're right. It nearly slipped my mind. And a party to introduce you to the community, Quinn. What a fine man Lochlan Balfour is."

"You're going then?"

"Oh, I wouldn't miss a chance to get inside the Devil's Keep."

I FELT EXCITED AND, truth to tell, a little nervous walking up to the castle entrance Saturday evening. It had seemed so distant and remote, like something out of a fairy tale, or at the very least a place that you'd pay twelve euro to get into and then have guides in every room telling you the history of the place. To come as an invited guest to an honest to goodness castle was kind of a thrill, even if the purpose was rather dark. We were out to unmask a killer.

I paused in front of the grand front door to gather myself. I touched my necklace of lapis, amethyst and black obsidian set in silver. A friend had given it to me the birthday when I was going through my divorce. The stones were for protection and clear communication, and I'd need plenty of both tonight.

Even though calling this a welcome party in my honor was a ruse, I still dressed as though I were the guest of honor. I wore a timeless little black dress that was the only proper dress-up outfit I'd brought with me. With it I wore black pumps and a purple and pink silk jacket. I'd spent extra time styling my hair and put on more makeup than I usually bothered with.

I pushed the bell for entry, and a woman wearing black trousers and jacket and a white blouse opened the door. Was she permanent staff, I wondered, or someone hired for the evening?

"Good evening, madam," she said.

"Good evening. I'm Quinn Callahan."

She smiled at me. "Mr. Balfour is expecting you. Please, head straight up the stairs and turn to your right."

I immediately started gawking like a tourist. The walls were stone and covered with tapestries that looked like the Flemish ones I'd seen in museums. They featured mythical creatures and well-dressed ladies.

I trod up the stone staircase and left the middle ages and entered modern times in a huge reception room.

While the castle was cold and forbidding on the outside, it was so different on the inside. Lochlan Balfour had kept the most interesting features, the huge fireplaces, where real wood fires were blazing, and the old windows, but then he'd added modern touches. The lighting was discreet but high-tech. The floors were gorgeous hardwood covered with rugs that even to my untutored eye looked like fancy Aubusson. The furniture was both luxurious and modern if you had to sit in it and rich-looking antiques if all you had to do was look at it. He'd hired a string quartet, which was playing music softly in the background already, even though no one was expected for half an hour yet.

Sean O'Grady had set up the food buffet and stood behind a wooden bar, looking very dapper in a waistcoat and white shirt.

Lochlan immediately came forward. He was wearing a dark blazer and flannels and a pale, gray shirt. The only thing colorful was that blood-red ruby when he extended his pale hand to welcome me. "How are you holding up? Are you ready?"

"As ready as I'll ever be." I glanced around and saw a few vampires, including the three from Oxford, chatting in soft voices. I noticed he'd kept the more colorful ones away, which I thought was an excellent plan.

He nodded. "I've never done this before either. I'm guessing the trick is not to rush our fences. Take your time."

"Do you think this will work?"

"Will the killer suddenly admit to their crime? I don't

know. All we can do is hope that if we prod the right people in the right spots, they'll start a chain reaction." He looked at me. "You have an idea who did it, don't you?"

"Honestly I'm not sure. I have some ideas. But I don't know. And I don't want to make a mistake. Imagine pointing the finger at the wrong murderer and then the real one goes free."

"I rather think that's what the real murderer's been doing so far. Sending pictures, planting knives and throwing everybody in different directions at once."

"I agree. So now, if we have everyone in one place and we get some truth-telling, who knows what will come out?"

The two detectives came in next. I knew that Lochlan was going to invite them, but I was surprised that they'd turned up. I walked over and said to DI Walsh, "Thank you for coming."

He looked around, and his tough-guy face nearly cracked a grin. "I admit, if it had been anywhere but the castle, I probably wouldn't have turned up. But how often do I get an invitation to get inside a place like this?"

It was so close to how I'd felt that I had to laugh. Though it was rather nervous laughter. "I know. And it's so much nicer inside than I could have imagined."

"Cost a few euro to update this place, that's for sure." He glanced around. "And even more to run it."

Then Lochlan Balfour came over and greeted them, and I was free to walk over to talk to Sean, the pub owner. "You've got the wine?"

He showed me the bottle. "I can see you're quite a fan. I'll have to order in some more."

He also had an array of little meat pies, cheese and crackers, vegetables and dip, fruit, some sandwiches, samosas and a nice tray of desserts, plus tea and coffee. I thought for whatever reason people were coming tonight, they wouldn't go home hungry. I asked for sparkling water as I wanted my wits about me.

I turned around and spotted Rafe Crosyer with Agnes Bartlett and Sylvia Strand. I walked over and greeted them. Like Lochlan, Rafe's style seemed to be vampire chic. The two older ladies had gone for designer older woman. Sylvia wore a set of diamonds that flashed richly in the light. Agnes Bartlett was more subdued, but still, I'd bet there was a designer label in that dress she was wearing. Her shoes looked to me like Prada. I hoped very much, when I was her age, I'd be as glamorous. And preferably not undead.

She said, "Don't be nervous, dear. Everything will turn out right. I'm convinced of it."

"Thank you," I said with real sincerity. "I'm as nervous as a kitten on hot coals."

"Well, metaphorically, that's exactly what you are," Rafe said. "You're an untried sleuth in company of a vicious murderer."

"Thank you. So comforting."

Sylvia told him off, and I drifted away. Already people were starting to arrive. They came in as wide-eyed as I had been. Within a very short time, it was clear that Lochlan had been right. No one was going to turn down an invitation to the castle. Eileen O'Connor and her son, Liam, came in together. Shortly behind her was Father O'Flanagan with the butcher, Sean Higgins, and Rosie. One look at the butcher's face suggested to me that he'd been dragged here unwillingly.

He looked like he'd rather be carving up dead carcasses than socializing. When he caught sight of DI Walsh and Sergeant Kelly, he looked like he might bolt.

Kate O'Leary, the schoolteacher, came in next with a pleasant-looking bald man who I assumed was her husband. Clearly he wasn't a reader, as we had never met. Karen Tate, who owned Granny's Drawers, came in together with Giles Murray, the photographer, and his girlfriend or wife, Beatrice.

Andrew Milsom came in wearing a jacket and tie and looking as though he'd rather be at home.

Kathleen McGinnis arrived, and Pendress Kennedy was with her. I didn't remember seeing Pendress's name on the invitation list, but she fit into the castle better than most. She looked so regal in her blue velvet skirt and jacket, embroidered with silver and gold threads, that she fit right in.

By seven o'clock, the room was full. Since nearly everybody here had known each other for years, it was amusing to watch them circulating socially, all wearing their best clothes and enjoying this opulent environment. I didn't think any of them had ever been in the castle before. I wondered how Lochlan felt now that his home had been invaded by the locals. I glanced at him, but his face was impassive. He was being the perfect host, circulating, greeting each guest.

Sean O'Grady was kept busy pouring drinks and inviting people to partake of the buffet. I made sure to stand very near the bar when each of the women I knew had been friendly with Declan came forward. I studied their faces as they were offered a glass of that special wine. Each of them reacted sharply.

Rosie Higgins's hand shook as she accepted a glass of the wine. She looked as though she might cry.

Karen Tate started and asked for white wine instead.

Kathleen accepted the wine and glanced at me as though knowing what I was up to. She raised her glass in my direction. *"Sláinte."*

Eileen O'Connor said, "Oh, no, thank you. I don't drink wine." He offered her whiskey or bottled beer, and she said, "If you've some sparkling water, that would be grand. Perhaps with a bit of lime."

Andrew Milsom came up and said, "You look nice."

I told him he did, too.

He sipped his whiskey. "I can't help but wonder what made the famously reclusive Lochlan Balfour open his castle to the great unwashed."

I chuckled and could hear how forced it sounded. "Everyone says he's a great benefactor of Ballydehag. Maybe he's just being nice."

"And yet the belle of the ball is visibly jumpy, the master of the keep is going out of his way to charm the locals, and he's serving very nice whiskey. I smell a plot."

He was too smart for his own good. Or mine. I made myself take a breath and with assumed casualness asked, "What plot?"

He glanced around. "I don't know. I suspect some sort of charity endeavor, perhaps, and we'll shortly be asked to take out our checkbooks."

At least he was a long way from the truth. I leaned closer. "Stick around."

"Oh, I intend to."

We let the party go on for a good half an hour until

everyone was settling in but hadn't had a chance to drink more than that first glass. We wanted them alert but relaxed. Lochlan waited until the string quartet had finished the current number and then clapped his hands. He was such a commanding figure, it didn't take thirty seconds before everyone was silent and looking at him. I had to swallow. I felt like my tongue was choking me. My heart was pounding, and my glass felt slippery in my grasp. This was the moment then.

Lochlan said, "Welcome everyone. Thank you for coming tonight. This little party is in honor of our newest resident of Ballydehag and the woman who's so competently running the town's bookshop. I admit, when Lucinda Corrigan left, I worried we'd lose the best bookshop this side of Dublin, but Quinn Callahan is doing a wonderful job."

There were murmurs of approval, and a couple of people said, "Hear, hear." Maybe they were only trying to be nice for their host's sake, but I still appreciated the support.

"Quinn, would you like to come forward and say a few words?"

No, Quinn would not. Quinn would rather be a million miles away. But Quinn had gotten herself into this mess by being so nosy and curious to solve the crime.

I was as bad as Cerridwen for poking my nose into dark corners, only Cerridwen had several lives. I had but the one.

Still, I pasted a happy smile on my face and went to stand beside Lochlan. He'd shifted the fancy high-tech lighting in such a way that everyone's face was illuminated.

"Thank you so much. I want to thank everyone for welcoming me to this beautiful village and for taking the time to come into the shop and get to know me. Of course, my first day here didn't go so very well. I walked into The

Blarney Tome and discovered Declan O'Connor murdered on the floor."

Some were still benignly smiling at me and nodding, but slowly, as my words sank in, the expressions changed to bewilderment. Discomfort. Guilt?

The murderer was here somewhere; I could feel the darkness like fog rolling in on a summer's day. I knew it in my witch's heart. I touched my necklace and hoped I was powerful enough to be able to unveil them.

Kathleen McGinnis and Pendress Kennedy were sending me strength. I could feel it. And I knew I was going to need it plus their extra intuition as well.

I continued, "I'd have liked to pretend it never happened, but for some reason, whoever killed Declan O'Connor has been pushing clues and information at me from the start. I don't know why. And if Declan's killer is here tonight, I really hope they'll explain themselves."

I looked around. There was dead silence and more than a little discomfort in the expressions. I watched a couple of people take steps backward, edging themselves toward the doorway. But we'd covered that eventuality. Rafe and Sylvia and Agnes had positioned themselves so that they were between the crowd and the door. No one would get out until the three vampires let them go. Rafe's power was obvious, but I suspected that if pushed, those two older women could kick ass.

"First, Eileen O'Connor and Liam, I'm sorry for your loss."

The baker's widow nodded, but she looked less than impressed that I was discussing her husband's murder at a social gathering.

"But it's very difficult to settle in this village knowing there's a killer at large. Because we all know someone in this village killed Declan O'Connor. And I believe that person is in this room now."

I heard a gasp. And then Giles Murray said, "Quinn, this is hardly cocktail party conversation."

"No. It isn't. But since we're all here, maybe we can help the police and hand them Declan O'Connor's killer. Wouldn't you like that, Giles? To know that Ballydehag is safe? You worry about Beatrice, don't you? You certainly keep her close."

"What on earth are you talking about?" He had his arm draped around her. He treated that woman like a fashion accessory. Now he pulled her closer. "Of course, I worry. Beatrice and I are devoted to each other."

I scanned the crowd. Andrew Milsom stood near the back, watching. He nodded slightly when my gaze landed on him.

I turned to Sean Higgins and Rosie. "Declan O'Connor came between you, didn't he? Rosie, you thought you were being so discreet, but someone saw you and Declan together."

"Quinn, how can you?" Rosie said in a choked voice.

I felt awful. I'd never thought, when I watched and read mysteries, that the big reveal at the end was so painful to do. People's feelings were hurt, their reputations damaged. But I'd come this far. I had to go on. "Who told you, Sean, about your wife and the baker?"

His face grew a dark, angry red. Like one of his own sirloin roasts. "I don't know what you're talking about. I didn't come here for this."

He took a step toward the exit, and Rafe subtly moved, making it clear he wasn't getting out of there without a fight. I could see he was thinking about it anyway. I stopped him with these words. "It was your butcher's knife that was used to slit Declan O'Connor's throat."

CHAPTER 28

Now he turned his fury onto me. "I've already told the police and anyone who cares to hear, the knife was missing. It's got my fingerprints all over it. Of course it does. It's my knife. The killer stole it from me and used it to murder Declan."

"And yet you never told the police your knife was missing. Not until it showed up in my bookstore covered in the victim's blood. Now, you've told me yourself that you're not a great reader. So how did your knife get into the bookstore? Unless you put it there. You knew your wife and Declan O'Connor were spending time together. I think you confronted him. You got him to meet you in the bookstore under some pretext. You had the key; it was easy enough. You're a big, heavy man. It wouldn't be hard to overpower the baker and kill him. Then what happened? Did you hear someone coming? You panicked and shoved the knife behind some books. I'm guessing you planned to come back for it but never got the chance."

He took a step toward me, and his fists were clenched.

Lochlan made a subtle move closer to my side. I'd stood my ground, but I still appreciated thinking that a big, strong vampire might stand in front of me before that overbuilt butcher went at me with his ham-fists.

"I didn't kill him. Yes, I knew he was having it off with my wife. Giles Murray told me."

The butcher's wife burst out crying. "Oh, what have I done? I'm sorry. I didn't mean to hurt you. But we were in love, you see. We were going to get married."

Her husband snorted. "Getting married, were ye? You were both already married."

She nodded, the tears running down her face now. "We were waiting until Liam was old enough. Then we were going to get married. We were going to ask you both for divorces."

I looked over at Karen Tate. She'd gone very pale, and her mouth was open. "That's not possible," she said. "Declan O'Connor was going to marry me."

Rosie Higgins stopped crying, and her eyes and mouth both opened wide. "What?"

"It's true. He loved me. You must be making this up." She glanced around. Like me, she'd gone for the little black dress, and as she moved, the light danced on her long, red hair, making it glow. "I'm single. And I was so lonely. Declan understood that. He used to come and fix little things that went wrong, just being a kind neighbor, but we fell in love."

"No. It's a lie," Rosie said.

Karen Tate continued. "I understood that he had to wait until his son was older. That's what a good man does. He fulfills his responsibilities, but as soon as Liam was old enough, he was planning to leave Eileen. But he was going to marry *me*."

Well, this was certainly going in a direction I hadn't anticipated.

I glanced at Kathleen. She looked shaken. I wasn't going to drag her into the public limelight like these two, because she'd known about Declan. It's bad enough when a mortal woman finds she's been made a fool of by a man, but when it happens to a witch, it's somehow worse. We're supposed to be so smart, so intuitive.

"Well," I said. "One of you killed him. Which one was it?"

The butcher's wife appealed to the detectives. "You've had my statement. You know I was home with my husband when the murder occurred. We were watching the television."

DI Murray had so far stayed in the background, but he spoke up now. "Your alibis are both for each other. Not the strongest I've ever heard. Either of you could be covering for the other one." He glanced at me. "Or they could have killed the man together. Trouble is, without proof, we're a bit stuck."

Karen Tate cried out, "But the bloody knife. Quinn said you've got a bloody knife with the victim's blood and the butcher's fingerprints all over it. What more do you need? A signed confession?"

He turned his cold gaze on her. "A signed confession would help, yes. Because otherwise, it's entirely circumstantial evidence. You'd best worry about your own alibi, miss."

"I was on the FaceTime with my cousin in Sweden," Karen protested. "I've told you that. She'll confirm it."

"Again, not the strongest of alibis, is it?"

"But—" She glanced around wildly. "But the photographs. The guards only questioned me because of an incriminating picture of me and Declan. Why would I push a picture that made me look guilty underneath the bookshop door? The murderer tried to frame me."

"Quite literally," I agreed. "I wondered why the photographs that had been printed out still seemed well-framed and the lighting was good enough that you could see the faces of the people even though they seemed like candid shots caught in a moment. That took quite a bit of skill. It fooled me at first, because the photographs looked like they'd been taken on a phone camera and printed off on a home computer. They looked amateur, but they weren't, were they, Giles?"

He looked around like a trapped animal staring down the barrels of a hundred rifles. "You're asking my professional opinion as a photographer? I haven't seen the photos in question."

"I think you have. I think you took them."

He spluttered and tried to look indignant, but it was all so clear to me now, I couldn't believe I hadn't seen it before.

"You're a photographer," I said. "Photographers observe. They record. This might be a small village, but it's a microcosm of the whole world. You said that yourself. And you were there behind the windows of your studio. Watching, recording. When did you decide to cause trouble? Were you just bored? Or did you want to teach Declan a lesson? You're obviously a jealous man. Maybe you were worried he'd go for Beatrice if you ever let that poor woman out from under your arm."

He took his arm away from Beatrice as though she had stabbed him with a pin. "I don't even know what you're accusing me of."

I was thinking as I was talking here, and I had to try and

get it all straight in my head. "I'm accusing you of taking those photographs. You pushed them under my door, but I'm beginning to think you somehow slipped them to Eileen too. That's how she found out her husband was stepping out on her."

"That's preposterous. Anyway, if I wanted to print things out, I've got a much higher quality printer to do it."

"I know. That fooled me, too. But then I remembered that everybody on the high street seems to have a key to everyone else's shop. How easy it was for you to slip into somebody else's store and print those photographs out."

"He promised he'd marry both of them?" Eileen seemed to be in a daze. She addressed her words to Giles, which made me suspect I'd been right. "You never told me that."

He shrugged. He was busted now, and he knew it. "I didn't know."

There was a tiny pause. I turned to Eileen O'Connor. "They all had motive, but you had the strongest of all, didn't you? Your husband was planning to leave you for another woman."

She looked white and pale and stunned. "I had no idea. Both of you? He promised to leave me for both of you? That means—" She clasped her hands together and let them go and then clasped them together again. She was squeezing so hard that the gold of her wedding ring seemed to push out from her skin as though it was unconnected to her.

"It means you didn't need to kill him after all," I said. "He wasn't really going to leave you. He kept putting them off, saying he had to wait until Liam was old enough, but Liam's grown up now. How old are you, Liam? Twenty-one?"

Liam was staring at his mother, but he answered quickly enough. "Twenty-two."

I continued addressing my words to Eileen. "I don't think Declan had any intention of leaving you. I think he strung those women along. Once they realized Liam was all grown up, he'd have come up with another excuse why he couldn't leave. Maybe he'd invent a disease for you, something that meant he could never be free. So, you see, you didn't need to kill him."

She shook herself as though she'd just got out of the shower. "I beg your pardon? Why would I kill my own husband? Besides, they may have weak alibis, but I've got a very strong one. Father O'Flanagan here will tell you. I was doing the flower arrangements at the church the night my husband was killed."

Father O'Flanagan nodded at me gravely. The man who'd been so cheerful and friendly in the bookstore now looked quite condemning. "It's true. Mrs. O'Connor was doing the flowers that evening. She couldn't have murdered her husband." He glanced at the two detectives. "And I hope you'll agree that I'm a very good alibi."

I shook my head. "But you didn't see her all the time. You told me yourself you were hearing confessions that night."

"But I came out every twenty minutes. I always do. I come out and greet my parishioners and have a look at their face, and then we go into the confessional. Every time I came out, Eileen was there and I saw the arrangement growing."

"You saw exactly what she wanted you to see." I turned back to Eileen. "In twenty minutes, you could easily get back to the bookshop, where you had invited your husband. Who did you tell him he was really meeting? Rosie? Karen?"

She was visibly shaken. Now she reached out and held on to her son's hand hard. "What you're suggesting is disgusting."

"What you did was disgusting. Not only did you murder your husband, but you kept trying to blame other people. Giles played right into your hands, pushing those photos under my door."

"I was trying to help," Giles protested. "I didn't want to get involved, but I thought the Guards should know about Declan's affairs."

I turned to the photographer. "It was Eileen you were helping. Once she knew you were giving evidence in that cowardly, anonymous way, she took the butcher's knife and hid it so clumsily that I was bound to find it. Rosie or Sean, she didn't mind who took the blame, so long as it wasn't her."

"This is crazy. Someone stop her," Eileen shouted.

No one did. I continued. "You got a bottle of the special wine he liked. I'm guessing you had the bottle open and uncorked on my cash desk with two empty glasses. Your husband came in. Was there a note saying, 'Meet me upstairs'? He'd have understood the signal. Probably poured two glasses of wine, and while he was doing that, you hit him on the back of the head. You stunned him. And then it was easy enough to slit his throat."

"No," she moaned.

"You thought you had all night to stage the scene, but you heard someone coming. So you panicked. You grabbed the wine and glasses, but you forgot the cork." I took it out of my pocket and held it up for everyone to see. Even though it was just a common, ordinary wine cork, several people gasped as though I'd pulled out a smoking gun. Though, in this case, this was the smoking gun.

"That's ridiculous. I don't even drink wine."

"I know. So why did you buy a bottle of *Vino d'Amour* two days before your husband died?"

I'd checked with Sean O'Grady to see who, apart from Declan, had bought Vino d'Amour that week, and he recalled Eileen O'Connor buying a bottle.

"It was a gift for Declan. He was the one who liked to drink wine. She sounded desperate and frightened and guilty.

"Mum. Shut up," her son suddenly said. He let go of her hand and stepped back.

"Liam. No. Darling boy. I'd do anything for you. Anything."

"Including murder," I said.

I had no more. If she didn't confess, I doubted there was enough evidence to convict her. I'd played my last card. Maybe I should have taken Lochlan's advice and paced myself better. Had I rushed in too fast with accusations? Would she get away with murder because I sucked at timing?

The painful silence lengthened. Everyone was looking at Eileen O'Connor and she was staring at her son.

And then Father O'Flanagan said one word. He said, "Eileen," in such a sorrowful, understanding tone that her face crumpled.

The man who'd been preaching from a pulpit more years than I'd been alive, probably, had something I lacked. He had great timing.

"I thought he was going to leave me for Rosie. I believed it." She glanced up, and her eyes glistened with unshed tears. "But he was promising both of them. If he told two women he was going to leave when his son grew up, that must have meant he had no intention of leaving at all."

I nodded to her. I had huge sympathy for this woman, but she had to pay for what she'd done. "While you were so busily arranging flowers, you overheard something in the confessional, didn't you?"

She nodded. "Rosie used to go in as regular as clockwork. After Giles showed me the picture ..." She glanced up at the priest. "I'm sorry, Father O'Flanagan. It was wrong of me, I know. I listened in on her confession and heard her telling you what she'd been up to. What they were planning."

If she thought eavesdropping was as bad as murder, she had a long way to go.

He took over now. "You must tell us now, my child. What did you do?"

"I heard her telling you that she'd been wrong. What they'd done. And then she said, almost as though it vindicated her, that he was going to leave us and marry her."

"I'm sorry," Rosie said, but I had no idea who she was apologizing to.

Eileen continued. "I didn't mind so much for myself. I knew there were times that he said he was at his sister's and he wasn't. I told myself to be patient, that it was a phase. He was teaching Liam to run the bakery. Everything is for Liam. All our hard work and the sacrifices, the holidays I've never had, the scrimping and saving, all of it was for Liam." She stopped and wiped her face with a cocktail napkin. "If he left us and married someone else? What would happen?"

She shook her head. "He'd be off spending all that money we'd worked for, that's what. Money that should have gone to his son. So I took a knife from next door. It was easy enough to do. We're in and out of each other's shops all the time. No one noticed.

"Of course, the bookshop was empty after Lucinda left. Meeting a woman there seemed like the sort of sly thing he might do. Take advantage like that. He seemed to buy an awful lot of bottles of wine, and I never saw him drinking them. I'd assumed he was saving them for Christmas, but after I found out about Rosie, I realized they were going at a quite regular rate. He had to be taking them to her. Them."

She looked at me. "That was clever of you, to work it out. You were right. I left him a message in Rosie's handwriting. We've known each other long enough I can write in her hand almost as well as my own. Good enough to fool my husband, anyway. I left him a note telling him to meet me, well, to meet Rosie at the bookshop. He knew I was at the church and the coast would be clear. I was at the church working on the flowers, but I had a nearly-finished arrangement and it was easy to swap it for the one I'd started, so it looked like I'd made progress when I hadn't even been there. I got to the bookshop and I hid behind one of the bookshelves. It was easy as anything. I left the wine and the glasses out, and he poured them. Two of them. He looked so pleased with himself. He was pouring the second glass when I came up behind him. I used a hammer from the shed. I did it like I was in a dream. One thing, then the other. I knew exactly how I had to do it."

She faltered. "And after ... I collected up the bottle and the glasses. I poured the wine down the sink and scrubbed it. I was nervous like. I heard footsteps approaching outside, so I ran out the back. I knew the cork was missing. But I thought no one would ever notice.

"I almost threw the knife away. But I thought no. Let Rosie

suffer the way I've suffered. Let her husband suffer the way I've suffered. Maybe if he'd been a better husband to her, she wouldn't have stepped out." Her words were rushing now, tripping over one another in her haste to get it all out. Her son stepped back, one step, two steps, three steps. Like he couldn't believe this was his mother.

"I couldn't understand why the police hadn't arrested Rosie yet. Or her husband. I was pleased then that I hadn't thrown away the knife. I planted it in your bookshop. I knew you'd find it sometime. Didn't imagine it would be so soon."

She didn't realize I had a super cat and a vampire on my team.

"It should be Rosie who's being arrested. Not me. She's the one who destroyed everything."

Father O'Flanagan came forward. "Come along now, Eileen. I'll get your coat."

He put an arm around her shoulders and turned to the two officers who were following. "If you could do the official business outside, it would be a kindness."

DI Walsh nodded, and the four of them left.

In the stunned silence that followed, Sean Higgins turned to his wife. "She's right, you know. It was you who destroyed everything."

"I thought he loved me," she said. Her husband stomped toward the door, and this time, nobody stopped him leaving. She looked around at the rest of us and then followed.

The party didn't go on for much longer after that. Giles Murray and Beatrice left, and everyone else soon followed. Andrew Milsom came up to me before he left. "Thank you for a very entertaining evening."

"At least you didn't have to get out your checkbook."

"No. Can I give you a lift home?"

"Oh." I felt a bit flustered. But he only wanted to make sure I got home safely. Or, more likely, to grill me for all the details of how I'd figured out who the murderer was. "I should help clear up," I said.

He nodded. "I'll see you around."

Sean O'Grady still stood behind his bar with the buffet table mostly still full of food. I walked over and helped myself to a square of cheese. I'd been too nervous to eat before.

"That's quite a party you throw," he said. "I've never seen anyone clear a room so fast."

I felt guilty for the pain I'd caused but also triumphant. Lochlan said, "You can go on home now yourself, Sean. My staff will tidy up."

He had staff to tidy up. Of course he did. He shook Sean's hand. "Thank you very much."

Sean laughed. "No. Thank *you*. This is the most excitement I've had since *Game of Thrones* ended. And almost as bloody."

Kathleen and Pendress waved on their way out.

When everyone had left except me and the vampires, Bartholomew was allowed to come out. "I was watching from the secret gallery up there," he said, sounding enthusiastic. "I couldn't have plotted that better myself, Quinn."

Rafe said, "He's right. Well done, Quinn. You handled that deftly."

I blew out a breath. I might have solved a murder but I'd made some enemies, too, in my new home. "I don't know about anybody else, but I could sure use a drink."

Agnes said, "There's plenty of *Vino d'Amour* left."

I shuddered. "I think I need something a little stronger."

"I've just the thing," Lochlan said. He went to a cabinet and withdrew a bottle. "This is a rather fine bottle of whiskey that I've been saving for a special occasion. I think this might be it."

He poured small glasses for all of us and said, "I was worried that life in Ballydehag was going to be too quiet and boring. And then Quinn Callahan arrived. You've brought more excitement among us in a couple of weeks than we'd had in the last two hundred years."

"Really?" I felt terrible.

"And for that we thank you." Then he raised his glass, and everyone else raised theirs. "To Quinn. Welcome to Ballydehag."

They all toasted me, and I said, on a laugh, "This won't happen again. From now on, I fully intend to lead a quiet, orderly life."

Lochlan Balfour shook his head. "Somehow, I doubt that's possible with you."

~

Thanks for reading *The Vampire Book Club!* I hope you enjoyed Quinn's adventure. Keep reading for a sneak peek of the next mystery, *Chapter and Curse,* Vampire Book Club Book 2.

~

Chapter and Curse, Chapter 1

"Are you not ready?" Kathleen McGinnis asked me, as she came into my bookshop.

I glanced up from unpacking a new order of books. "Ready for what?"

My sister witch was more dressed up than usual, wearing a flowered dress with a pale blue cardigan. She'd also curled her hair and sported fresh lipstick. She clucked her tongue against the roof of her mouth. "Billy O'Donnell's wake, of course."

"Why would I go to Billy O'Donnell's wake? I barely knew the man."

"He was a customer here for years."

"But I've been here for less than a month." I thought Billy O'Donnell had bought some books on Roman history, but that could have been Billy O'Connell. In fact, I wasn't completely sure which one of them was dead.

"It's a mark of respect. Everyone in Ballydehag will be there. Besides, it's a chance for you to meet a few people. Get them to know and trust you."

After I'd exposed a murderer, and a few dark secrets of this small town along the way, I felt people looking at me askance, like they were pleased to have a murderer caught, but not sure about the collateral damage. Kathleen was right, the more time I spent socializing with my new neighbors, the sooner they'd lower their guard around me. At least I hoped so. "But who will look after my shop?"

She shook her head at me. "There won't be any business. Everybody in town will be at Billy O'Donnell's."

I looked down at my jeans and blue silk shirt. "Can I go home and change?"

"No, no. There's no time. Here, this'll do."

She dashed to where I had a sweater hanging on a hook. It had been there for a couple of weeks. It was black and hip-length and I didn't want to wear it as today was a warm spring day. I'd be sweltering. Still, I did as I was told and put the sweater on. She stood back and nodded. "It's a shame about the jeans. Never mind. Everyone knows you're an American."

Then, I am not kidding, she pulled a pink plastic comb from out of her capacious handbag and tidied up my hair. As though she were my grandmother. I waited for her to spit on her hankie and wipe my face, but luckily she didn't go that far. Then she stood back, looking quite pleased with herself. "There. That'll do. Now come along, we don't want to be late."

I really doubted Billy O'Donnell was going to notice if we were late or not.

Order your copy today! *Chapter and Curse* is Book 2 in the Vampire Book Club series.

A Note from Nancy

Dear Reader,

Thank you for reading the *Vampire Book Club.* It was such a joy to write. I hope you'll consider leaving a review and please tell your friends who paranormal women's fiction and cozy mysteries. Review on Amazon, Goodreads or BookBub.

If you enjoy paranormal cozy mysteries, you might also enjoy the *Vampire Knitting Club* - a story that NYT Bestselling Author Jenn McKinlay calls "a delightful paranormal cozy mystery perfectly set in a knitting shop in Oxford, England. With intrepid, late blooming amateur sleuth, Lucy Swift, and a cast of truly unforgettable characters, this mystery delivers all the goods."

Join my newsletter for a free prequel, *Tangles and Treasons*, the exciting tale of how the gorgeous Rafe Crosyer, from The Vampire Knitting Club series, was turned into a vampire.

I hope to see you in my private Facebook Group. It's a lot of fun. www.facebook.com/groups/NancyWarrenKnitwits

Until next time,
Happy Reading,

Nancy

ALSO BY NANCY WARREN

The best way to keep up with new releases, plus enjoy bonus content and prizes is to join Nancy's newsletter at NancyWarrenAuthor.com or join her in her private Facebook group Nancy Warren's Knitwits.

Vampire Book Club: Paranormal Women's Fiction Cozy Mystery

Crossing the Lines - Prequel

The Vampire Book Club - Book 1

Chapter and Curse - Book 2

A Spelling Mistake - Book 3

Vampire Knitting Club: Paranormal Cozy Mystery

Tangles and Treasons - a free prequel for Nancy's newsletter subscribers

The Vampire Knitting Club - Book 1

Stitches and Witches - Book 2

Crochet and Cauldrons - Book 3

Stockings and Spells - Book 4

Purls and Potions - Book 5

Fair Isle and Fortunes - Book 6

Lace and Lies - Book 7

Bobbles and Broomsticks - Book 8

Popcorn and Poltergeists - Book 9

Garters and Gargoyles - Book 10

Diamonds and Daggers - Book 11

Herringbones and Hexes - Book 12

Ribbing and Runes - Book 13

Cat's Paws and Curses - A Holiday Whodunnit

Vampire Knitting Club Boxed Set: Books 1-3

Vampire Knitting Club Boxed Set: Books 4-6

The Great Witches Baking Show: Culinary Cozy Mystery

The Great Witches Baking Show - Book 1

Baker's Coven - Book 2

A Rolling Scone - Book 3

A Bundt Instrument - Book 4

Blood, Sweat and Tiers - Book 5

Crumbs and Misdemeanors - Book 6

A Cream of Passion - Book 7

Cakes and Pains - Book 8

Gingerdead House - A Holiday Whodunnit

The Great Witches Baking Show Boxed Set: Books 1-3

Toni Diamond Mysteries

Toni is a successful saleswoman for Lady Bianca Cosmetics in this series of humorous cozy mysteries.

Frosted Shadow - Book 1

Ultimate Concealer - Book 2

Midnight Shimmer - Book 3

A Diamond Choker For Christmas - A Holiday Whodunnit

Toni Diamond Mysteries Boxed Set: Books 1-4

The Almost Wives Club

An enchanted wedding dress is a matchmaker in this series of romantic comedies where five runaway brides find out who the best men really are!

The Almost Wives Club: Kate - Book 1

Secondhand Bride - Book 2

Bridesmaid for Hire - Book 3

The Wedding Flight - Book 4

If the Dress Fits - Book 5

The Almost Wives Club Boxed Set: Books 1-5

Take a Chance series

Meet the Chance family, a cobbled together family of eleven kids who are all grown up and finding their ways in life and love.

Chance Encounter - Prequel

Kiss a Girl in the Rain - Book 1

Iris in Bloom - Book 2

Blueprint for a Kiss - Book 3

Every Rose - Book 4

Love to Go - Book 5

The Sheriff's Sweet Surrender - Book 6

The Daisy Game - Book 7

Take a Chance Boxed Set: Prequel and Books 1-3

Abigail Dixon: A 1920s Cozy Historical Mystery

In 1920s Paris everything is très chic, except murder.

Death of a Flapper - Book 1

For a complete list of books, check out Nancy's website at
NancyWarrenAuthor.com

ABOUT THE AUTHOR

Nancy Warren is the USA Today Bestselling author of more than 100 novels. She's originally from Vancouver, Canada, though she tends to wander and has lived in England, Italy and California at various times. While living in Oxford she dreamed up The Vampire Knitting Club. Favorite moments include being the answer to a crossword puzzle clue in Canada's National Post newspaper, being featured on the front page of the New York Times when her book Speed Dating launched Harlequin's NASCAR series, and being nominated three times for Romance Writers of America's RITA award. She has an MA in Creative Writing from Bath Spa University. She's an avid hiker, loves chocolate and most of all, loves to hear from readers!

The best way to stay in touch is to sign up for Nancy's newsletter at NancyWarrenAuthor.com or join her private Facebook group facebook.com/groups/NancyWarrenKnitwits

To learn more about Nancy and her books
NancyWarrenAuthor.com

facebook.com/35585383469
twitter.com/nancywarren1
instagram.com/nancywarrenauthor
amazon.com/Nancy-Warren/e/B001H6NM5Q
goodreads.com/nancywarren
bookbub.com/authors/nancy-warren

Printed in Great Britain
by Amazon